LAST
RESORT

A Willow Bay novel

by Laurie Ryan

www.laurieryanauthor.com

Editor: Libby Doyle, Fairhill Editing
Cover design by Visual Node for Graphics

Learn more about Laurie Ryan and her books at
www.laurieryanauthor.com and for up-to-date
information about releases, please consider joining Laurie's
mailing list through her website.

QUALITY CONTROL: We strive to produce error-free
books, but even with all the eyes that see the story during
the production process, slips get by. So please, if you find a
typo or any formatting issues, please let us know at
laurie@laurieryanauthor.com so that we may correct it.
Thank you!
.

Dedication

To Char, Kathy, Trudy, and Rachal, the best sisters ever.

Chapter One

"Where is she?" Josh Morgan muttered as he stared across the rain-drenched street, his gut churning. Dana opened her shop every single day, and on time. Well, mostly. He glanced at his watch. Almost noon. She was two hours late.

The streets were empty except for pools of water and the constant barrage of Mother Nature's rainspout. Not a moving car in sight. Even the quaint C&C Coffee Shop where Josh waited was devoid of customers, except for him. Welcome to February at the beach in Washington.

"Looking for someone, mayor?"

Connie, the café's owner, filled his coffee mug. Setting the pot on the table, she plunked into the booth across from Josh with an oomph, shoulders rounded and worry lines etching her face. She looked older than her forty-five years and the short brown hair that framed her face showed touches of gray.

"I noticed the gift shop isn't open yet."

"Look around. Nothing is, except me. Too much rain, too few tourists."

Focused on Dana's shop, Josh hadn't noticed the other stores on the little strip. Connie was right. Everything was closed. Not unusual for a Monday, unless you were Dana Ricci.

"She's open every day, though. Maybe I should check on her." Except he didn't know where she lived. Josh reached for his coffee.

Connie grinned. "Why, mayor, if I didn't know better, I'd say you were sweet on that girl."

The cup hit the table with a thunk, coffee sloshing over the sides. Her statement hit a little too close to home. Josh willed himself to stare Connie down, to keep his face bland and emotionless. He broke first, looking back out the window toward the gift store. Damn it.

Connie stood and reached for a rag to wipe up Josh's mess. "Oh, yeah, you're in deep." She laughed and tossed the rag back in the pail.

Josh hated to admit it, but she was right. All the promises, all the talks he'd had with himself after Sandra left him had flown straight out the window when he'd met the dark-haired gift shop owner. He'd fought it, and still tried to, but his damn heart wouldn't budge. Neither would other parts of him. Dana was full of life, zest, and happiness. He was drawn to her like numbers to a spreadsheet. Damn. He was in so much trouble.

"You want anything to eat?" Connie asked, still grinning.

"Not yet. I'm waiting for someone."

"Who you meeting up with?"

"Some guy who wants to propose, well, something. I'm not sure what. Said he wanted to talk in person." Josh hadn't liked how vague Alexander Granson had been on the phone. He'd googled the man, an architect with a lot of grand ideas, and Josh had first-hand experience with his type. He grimaced.

Granson didn't seem like a good fit for the town. Small

even by oceanside community standards, Willow Bay snugged up to dunes filled with grasses and willow, had beaches that seemed to go on forever, and curved with the land around a somewhat sheltered alcove of the Pacific Ocean. But with mid-winter just behind them, the town was hurting. Most tourists wanted sunshine when they came to the beach. They wanted to play, to shop, to listen to the ocean's grandeur as it crashed upon the shore. This winter, the coast had been inundated with rain, not a big enough draw even for storm-watchers. As mayor, and the only accountant in town, he had first-hand knowledge of how much Willow Bay needed people to come visit and spend money.

He owed it to the people who lived here to listen to any ideas that would increase tourism and revenue, so he'd agreed to meet the man.

"Do you think he has a plan to boost things here?"

Josh shrugged. "I won't know until I talk to him."

"It would be nice if someone did something to help."

Connie Lassiter didn't have a mean bone in her body, so Josh tried to take her comment for what it was. Frustration and worry.

"I'm doing what I can."

"Ah, I'm sorry, Josh." Connie patted his shoulder like she was placating one of her three children. "I know you are. You're sure a darn sight better than old Ben. Change never set right with him. Neither did the opinions of the people here. You care and it shows. I'm just...worried."

"Charlie still not working?"

"In this rain? Not much construction going on when you have to work in the mud." She stood, straightened, and shook her head. "Another month or so and things will pick up."

"Yes, they will," Josh said, trying to stay positive as he

noted how her hand trembled.

"Yep. Just holler when you're ready to order."

"I will. Thanks, Connie. And hang in there."

"I always do, mayor," she said with a non-committal wave of her hand as she headed toward the kitchen. "I always do."

Turning back to the window, he watched the steady rainfall. Long-range forecasts indicated another couple weeks of this, then a gradual change over to spring and a warmer than usual summer. Willow Bay just needed to hold out until then. The tourists would return. They always did.

He glanced again at the gift shop, still not open. *Where is she?*

~~~

"Is this some sort of joke?" Dana Ricci sank onto her bed as she stared at the letter in her hands. Fancy stationery from some attorney in New York, saying she owed almost $200,000. She'd never even been to New York.

• *Condo rental totaling $130,000.*
• *A secured loan for $70,000.*

Someone had stolen her identity. That had to be the reason. She sure didn't need this right now. Her gift shop teetered on a financial cliff that was getting worse, not better. How could someone have racked up this much debt in her name without her knowing it? How could she find out? Call the attorney? No. She didn't want him to have her phone number, to be able to find her. Dana picked up the envelope sent to her gift shop, realizing that ship had sailed.

Duffy, her perennially happy Beagle/Yorkie mix, whined. Dana scratched his ears as she read the letter again.

Make payment arrangements or we will advise our client to pursue foreclosure proceedings on Tangerine Treasures.

The gift shop she'd sunk the last of her money into six months ago. That she loved, despite how hard it was to make a go of things. She looked around her one-room "apartment" at the back of the store. She'd brought her comfy bed with her. A window at the back made it less claustrophobic. A dresser, clothes rack, and a long table held all her worldly possessions—including her food, a microwave, and a coffee pot—with a small fridge snuggled beneath it. She didn't need a T.V. She had wifi and a tablet for what little she watched. And the shop's bathroom had a shower in it.

Willow Bay had saved her after Jett had split to follow some wanderlust she'd never understood.

"I'm going with or without you," her husband had said. "I'm meant for more than this Podunk town."

"Spokane is a city, not a town," she'd argued. "And it's pretty big in its own right."

"Well, it's not big enough for me. I want more. I thought you did, too."

Two years later, his departure still stung. She'd been dazzled by him, swept off her feet right up until he drove their finances into the ground, overextending them on everything. Even then, she couldn't look into those dark, soulful eyes of his and rebuke him.

Oh, God. Could it be? Dana glanced at the stack of papers on top of her dresser. Her divorce papers were in there, not yet finalized because she had no way to contact Jett to get his signature. His cell had been disconnected and he'd never given her an address. She read the letter a third time, glancing at the itemized list. Was there a chance this wasn't just a scam? She had to know for certain, so Dana reached for her phone.

Please, don't let this be more of Jett's foolishness.

When she hung up with the attorney's office, Dana's grip on the letter loosened and it floated to the ground. She followed it, sinking off the bed to the floor, her long, dark hair falling forward, her hands covering her face.

It was true. Jett had accrued these debts by taking out credit in her name. He'd destroyed her. The man who'd wooed her until she married him, who wouldn't take no for an answer. He'd loved her, or so she thought. How could he do this to someone he'd said he loved?

Dana had tried to argue with the collection attorney, but he'd shut her down with one question.

"Was the divorce ever finalized, Mrs. Sanders?"

No matter that she'd reverted to her maiden name. That was a legality that bill collectors didn't care about. They knew she hadn't filed the divorce papers yet. They had her right where they wanted her.

And she was totally screwed.

Chapter Two

The red Lexus IS convertible that pulled into a parking spot at the café looked very out of sync with the rain that pounded its canvas roof. The driver got out and raced into the restaurant. He slipped out of his charcoal gray trench coat and shook it, sending droplets of water everywhere. He held the coat at arm's length and looked around, finally laying it over the first booth.

Taking a moment to run his hands over dark hair that didn't show a strand out of place, he saw Josh and his frown changed to a dazzling smile.

"Mayor Morgan?"

Josh nodded and the man joined him, glancing at the vinyl booth bench before sitting down and extending his hand. "Alexander Granson."

The man didn't have a wimpy handshake. There was some muscle behind it in direct contrast to the city-boy look of him.

"Would you like something to drink, to eat?" Josh said, handing him a menu.

"Definitely. I drove straight through from Seattle."

Josh waved Connie over.

Granson searched quickly. "Any decent coffee?"

"I can manage most anything."

"Great. Double espresso for me. And I'll have a turkey sandwich, hold the bread and condiments. And no sides, please."

Connie wrote the order down with no hint of surprise except one raised eyebrow and turned to Josh.

"A BLT for me, with everything."

"Got it." She glanced at Granson, then headed behind the counter and went to work.

"A bit of rain today, isn't there?"

Josh snorted. "Yes. A bit."

"Is this normal?"

"For this time of year, yes. There may be more than usual right now, but this is winter on the Washington coast."

Connie set a cup and saucer in front of Granson, who sniffed the espresso with appreciation, turning his gilded smile her way. "This smells heavenly. Thank you."

The owner of the C&C Coffee Shop had dealt with some characters over the years, and Josh had never once seen her lose her cool. Or blush. Until now. Color filled Connie's cheeks.

"Anytime," she said, shoving her hands in her pockets. "Let me know if you'd like another." This time, when she left, she walked more slowly and turned back once to stare at Josh's guest.

Josh shook his head and refocused on the man across the booth from him. "So, what brings you here, Mr. Granson?"

"Alex, please. I'm going to become Willow Bay's new best friend. I have an opportunity to share that I think you'll absolutely love. One that will bring this place from the brink of extinction to the best known oceanside town on the west coast."

"The whole coast?"

"Yes."

"That's a pretty bold statement."

Granson nodded. "One that I can back up."

Grandiose schemes didn't mesh well with Josh's practical nature, and he had a very strong feeling this man's ideas would approach or surpass lofty. He could see Connie watching them as she made sandwiches, or one sandwich and one...hell, he didn't even know what to call a turkey sandwich without the bread. He did have a word for the expression on Connie's face, even from this distance. Hope.

So while Josh would prefer to send Alexander Granson on his way after a free lunch, he owed it to Willow Bay to hear the man out.

"All right," Josh said, gripping his coffee cup and looking the man in the eye. "Tell me your plan."

He didn't answer right away because Connie set their food in front of them.

"Anything else I can get you?" she asked.

Granson turned that thousand-watt smile on her again. "No. This is perfect. Thank you."

With obvious reluctance, she headed back behind the counter to wipe it down, something she'd done just before the man had walked in. The counter didn't need to be cleaned again, but the task kept Connie within hearing distance. Josh shook his head. Nothing stayed secret for long in this town.

After slicing his turkey non-sandwich and chewing a couple bites, Granson spoke up. "I've all but secured the rights to the land behind the town hall."

"You mean the old cannery?"

"And the land surrounding it, just shy of two hundred acres."

Josh's gut began to churn. Whatever this was, it sounded big. "What could you possibly do with that much land?"

"Build a resort that will make those California parks seem small by comparison."

Josh had expected big, but not that big. He didn't even know where to start with his questions. The idea overwhelmed him, and not in a good way. He'd been to theme parks. All cement and crowds and citified atmosphere. Willow Bay's small-town appeal would be swallowed up.

"That sounds like a lot more than Willow Bay can handle," he said slowly, then took a bite of BLT that now tasted like cardboard.

"This will put you on the map. People will come from all over the world. Places like this coffee shop will finally be able to thrive."

"I think it's a fine idea," Connie said, joining them.

"There's a lot to consider here, Connie." Irritation flooded Josh. The Willow Bay gossip line traveled faster than lightning. He should have met this guy at the office. He needed time to think about this, to do his due diligence on Granson.

"It's stopped raining," Granson said, signaling Connie. "Can I have this wonderful coffee to go, please?" He turned back to Josh. "Let's take a walk. Show me your town and I'll flesh out my idea for you." He didn't wait for an answer but stood and reached for his coat. "I'm sure you'll love it when you hear more." He thanked Connie for the food he barely ate.

The way Connie responded, Josh could tell he'd have his work cut out for him if this idea wasn't a good fit for Willow Bay. She didn't hear Josh ask for a box for his BLT until he said it a second time.

He paid the bill, shrugged on his yellow slicker, and followed the man out the door, wondering when he'd gotten so cynical about change.

~~~

For the first time in her life, Dana was at a loss over how to proceed. If she truly was liable for this debt, she'd need to figure out some sort of payment plan that didn't extend for about a bazillion years past her gravestone placement. Something that would placate the lawyers until she could sort everything out. Speaking of which, she'd need to talk to an attorney. Not Michaels. He might be the only attorney in Willow Bay and have excellent credentials, but she absolutely did not want this to get out and jeopardize the fragile friendships she'd so recently formed here.

Though how long could she stay if she wasn't making any money? She'd switched the gift shop's door sign from closed to open, but even as the rain abated, she knew there would be no customers again today. Not on a Monday, in February, with more rain on the way.

She could clean houses before and after work. Except most people didn't want their houses cleaned at four in the morning or while they were eating dinner. Maybe she could clean offices at night. That might work.

Had she seen a help wanted sign at the grocery store? She'd have to ask Sam, the owner.

She could walk dogs.

She could... Hell, none of these jobs would make her the kind of money she needed. She'd have to sell her body at a very high price to even make a dent.

Dana looked around at the aisles, full of *gingilli*, her grandmother's word for knick-knacks. She had snow-globes and ceramics, screen-printed shirts, and flip-flops. The corner she'd designated for local artisans had become her pride and joy. The best blackberry jam she'd ever tasted. Locally made taffy in more flavors than she could imagine. And their local celebrity, Shiri, had given her several paintings on consignment. They adorned one entire tangerine-painted wall.

Cupping her chin in her hand while she leaned on the cashier counter, Dana stared at the closest painting, her favorite. A sunny day at the beach, with a swirl of seagulls coming in for a landing on the sand, the ocean beside them. Just a hint of willow and dunes off in the distance. A part of her wished it would never sell so she could keep staring at it. Dana didn't have an artistic bone in her body, though she loved the imaginations of others and was proud to support that in some small way.

She turned back to the wall of windows filled with items to entice folks to enter and shop. Nothing moved except rainwater falling from the gutter. All of her hard work over these past few months might get flushed down the storm drain with the winter rains.

Make payment arrangements or we will pursue foreclosure proceedings on Tangerine Treasures.

Damn Jett anyhow. How could he do this? Especially to someone he supposedly loved. Or had at one time. Dana's wounded heart hurt more than it should. She was over him, except... the idea of him lingered. They'd had some fun times. He'd been so vivacious, so capable of stealing her heart. She'd worked hard to get her equilibrium back, only to have him steal everything else.

Dana needed an attorney, and for more reasons than one. She stared at the envelope under the receipts now spread across her counter. She would get divorced whether she could find Jett or not. The New York attorney had said they had no idea where her husband-in-name-only was, that he'd disappeared. She'd wanted to be nice and make sure he knew the divorce would be filed. That plan had certainly come back to haunt her.

Aimi. She needed to call her best friend back in Spokane. Aimi was an attorney. She did family law. Surely, she'd be able to advise her.

And she'd need an accountant. Willow Bay's serious-but-cute mayor came to mind. He juggled the town and his own business better than she ever could. Josh Morgan stopped by most days to say hi and she'd come to treasure those times. He probably visited all the shops, but Dana looked forward to seeing him, with his dusty blond hair and those light blue eyes that seemed to see right through to her soul. Always organized, always calm. She'd wondered more than she should about whether or not there was some fire under that calm, quiet façade. And if she could be the one to find out.

Shaking her head, she looked down at the receipts, the letter from New York, the manila envelope with her unfiled divorce papers in it. Josh Morgan had his life completely together while hers was falling apart.

No, now wasn't the time for fantasies. Now, she needed to make plans. Dana tugged on her ponytail.

God help her if she couldn't find a way out of this mess.

Chapter Three

Five years ago, shortly after moving to Willow Bay, Josh had learned that the right pair of shoes meant everything in a northern, oceanside community. He wore mostly boots now, at least in winter. Waterproof boots.

"Nice shoes," he said to Granson.

"Thank you. Gucci."

Granson skirted yet another puddle while Josh walked right through it, smothering his smile.

"Is it always this wet around here?"

Josh shrugged. "Not in August. Usually not September. Oh, and half of July."

They'd reached the corner. Willow Bay's main roads paralleled the shoreline, with bisecting streets that fanned out like a wagon wheel. One block ahead of them stood the unassuming one-story building that housed police, fire, and Josh's tiny mayor's office, though he handled most things from his accounting business. Beyond that, other than the sunken shell of the cannery, the mostly undeveloped terrain was full of willow trees. A backdrop of nature that guarded the town's rural feel.

Granson stopped, waving his hands at the expanse. "Just imagine what this could be, instead of the rusticity people see now when they come to town."

Josh bristled. "People expect that *rusticity*."

"Some do. But imagine, on a day like today, an indoor playground. Spray and water parks for the kiddies, bars and restaurants for the adults."

"And a casino?" Josh threw out the question to test the man's reaction, given that casinos were only legal on tribal lands.

"Maybe a small one."

Josh stared at him. How could he possibly think he could build a casino in a state whose laws only allowed them on sovereign land?

"Just imagine," Granson went on, oblivious to Josh's expression. "A multi-story hotel filled with amenities. Perfect views of the ocean from every room. And, for those fair-weather days, an outdoor theme park."

Josh tried to picture it, tried to see the benefits. Yes, it would bring in people. Lots of people, the kind who liked to spend money. The kind of help sorely needed here. But all he imagined was flashing lights and the loss of perfect night skies to stargaze. Moonlit water would disappear beneath the come-hither glare of Granson's resort. And the small-town ambiance of Willow Bay would be changed, probably forever.

Granson clapped a hand on Josh's shoulder, startling him from the reverie.

"I can see you're not convinced."

"I'm here to do what's best for the town," Josh said, moving out from under his hand.

"Help it make money! Isn't that what's needed to bring Willow Bay back from the edge?"

"It's part of what's needed."

"It's the part I'm here to make happen."

"But is it the right image for us?" Josh couldn't imagine

how it would be.

"It's the right image for any town." Granson glanced at the strip mall across the street. "Come on. Let's go find someone to talk to about this. Start getting the opinions of the people who live and work here."

"I live and work here," Josh said.

"Yes. And I did some checking on you. Seems you like to get town input on decisions. So come on. Let's start looking for that approval." He didn't wait for an answer. He shot across the street, ducking under the awning that ran the length of the strip as the rain returned in earnest.

Josh pulled the hood of his slicker up and followed at a more careful pace, watching as Granson tried the first door, peered in the window, then moved to the next shop. He tossed his cup of coffee toward a garbage can. He missed it completely, almost clocking Gladys, their resident street-person, in the head. Granson paid no attention, but Josh hurried to the old lady's side.

"You okay, Gladys?" he said, steadying her. Very little sign of her white hair showed beneath the wool cap she wore. He could swear she had on about three layers of clothes with a mud-spattered slicker covering it all.

"I'm fine. Thank you." She smiled up at him. "Who's the asshole?"

Good old Gladys, calling things as she sees them.

"Someone who thinks he knows what's good for Willow Bay." Josh reached down for the errant coffee cup, putting it in the garbage can Granson had missed.

"Hmpf. His kind don't know what Willow Bay needs."

"Not sure I disagree with you, but I have to hear him out."

Gladys gripped him with her gloved hand, surprising him with her strength. "As mayor, you have to do what's best for this town."

Shit. First Granson intimates Josh can't make a decision on his own, then Gladys takes him to task. Damn it. He was doing the best he could. Didn't good leaders get opinions? "I'm trying," he muttered.

"Ah, I know you are, Joshua. I know you are." She loosened her grip and patted his arm. "Just don't let that kind of person sweet-talk you into something this town don't need."

"I won't. I promise." Josh watched as the man in question slipped inside Tangerine Treasures. Dana must have opened. Relief and worry collided in his stomach, an epic storm. Why had she opened so late? He needed to be in that shop now. Still, before following after the businessman, he turned to Gladys. "Another soaker today. You want me to give you a ride over to the shelter?"

"Nah. I don't need no shelter. I've got my slicker and my rain hat, and everything else I need is in Mabel here."

Mabel. The tarp-covered grocery cart she pushed around. Josh had tried numerous times to help her set down roots somewhere. Some people just didn't want to be settled. "You need anything? Have you eaten today?"

"Not yet, but I'm about to. Look." She reached under the tarp and pulled out a half-full bag of potato chips. "Found these in the trash. Perfectly good. It's amazing what some people throw out. Found a bunch of cans, too. Turning those in will get me my dinner tonight."

Josh chuckled. She was a scrapper, this one. "All right, but you've got my number. You need anything, you have someone call me. And here." Josh handed her the BLT he'd barely touched.

"Thank you, mayor," she said, taking the box. "But you'd better get after that city boy and keep him out of our business."

She tucked the food under her tarp and ambled off,

pushing Mabel right out into the rain and onto her chosen destination. Josh watched her until she rounded the corner, then he turned and raced down the sidewalk, pushing his way through the door into one of his favorite places in Willow Bay. Alexander Granson leaned on the counter close to the shop's beautiful owner. Beautifully frazzled, that is, as Duffy—clutched in Dana's arms—growled and bared his teeth at Granson.

Josh smiled.

I knew I liked that dog.

~~~

Dana had no sooner quieted the normally reticent Duffy, than the shop's bell pealed again, sending the dog into another tizzy. This time, he leaped from her arms before she could react and launched himself with happy abandon toward the front door. Josh squatted and took the small dog's weight full force as they collided. Duffy yipped and licked Josh's face until Dana barked at him to behave. Duffy, tail spinning like crazy, loped back behind the counter, with one final growl for Granson as he went.

"Blanket, Duffy. Now." Dana pointed at the dog bed nestled behind the counter. Duffy looked at her, then glared at the man leaning over the counter.

"Duffy!"

Stuffing his tail between his legs, Duffy settled on the cushion, baring his teeth one last time before putting his head down and going from amped up to nap time in a matter of three seconds. Four, tops.

"Hi, Josh," Dana said, running her hands through her hair. She knew she looked a mess. With the nosedive her morning had taken, she hadn't spruced up before opening. Dana hated looking anything less than ideal in front of Willow Bay's handsome mayor. Nothing to do about that now. She pasted on her friendliest smile and turned back to the gentleman still leaning on her counter.

"I'm sorry about my dog, sir. He's normally very friendly with customers."

The man, handsome in a slick, perfect mold sort of way, glanced over the counter and down at Duffy. "Kind of a liability waiting to happen, isn't he?"

Dana's smile slipped a notch. She buried the long breath she wanted to take. "Duffy's a good dog, and as you can see, he does mind what I say." *Some of the time.* "Most people love him. I truly am sorry he didn't take to you."

"He took out after me."

"He doesn't bite."

"You can't promise that."

"Well, he's a rescue dog and has had most of his teeth removed, so yes, I pretty much can."

Who was this guy? Sure, he was good-looking, in an Armani sort of way, but he didn't seem like the type to visit a small gift shop in the middle of a downpour in winter. At the ocean. An image of her ex walking on the beach in the pouring rain came to mind. Yeah, that would never happen.

Still, a customer is a customer and Dana pasted her proprietor smile back on her face. "How can I help you?"

Josh joined them at the counter. The man nodded to him, then faced Dana, his smile transforming his face from upper-crust judgmental to, well... Wow. The man was really handsome when he smiled, very GQ and friendly and...perfect, from his dark, nicely cut and styled hair to the stark contrast of perfect white teeth without a single blemish.

He held out his hand. "I'm sorry. I never introduced myself. I'm Alexander Granson. Call me Alex, please."

Warmth enveloped her hand as they shook. Warmth and smoothness. Dana tried to pull her own work-roughened hands back, wishing she'd thought to put lotion on them this morning.

"I'm Dana Ricci, Mr.—Alex. Owner of this shop. It's a pleasure to meet you. Is there something I can help you find?"

He hadn't yet let go of her hand. "I think I've just found what I came looking for."

Josh was looking damn near apoplectic, his face turning different shades of red as the man held her hand. Could he be jealous of this guy? That was hard to believe. In the six months she'd been in the town, he'd never asked her out or suggested anything beyond friendship. Was it awful of her to want to test her theory and maybe shake things up a bit?

"And what are you looking for, Mr. Gran, uh, Alex?" Trying to bat her lashes, Dana was quite certain she looked more like a person with itchy pink eye than a vixen, but hopefully Josh hadn't seen that.

"Why, your beauty, of course." He kissed her hand. "It's nice to know this backwoods town has something going for it."

Dana had loved Willow Bay and its people from the moment she'd arrived. Bristling at the backwoods comment, Dana pulled her hand carefully from Alex's gentle grip, her smile disappearing. No one insulted her town. Before she could retort, she noticed the death-grip Josh had on the counter. He didn't like Alexander Granson, either.

Maybe she could break that stiff upper lip of Josh's yet, though to do it with Mr. Slick didn't appeal to her much. She'd sure like to get Josh to relax and talk to her more, though. She'd hinted several times. She'd like other things, too, things that sometimes kept Dana awake at night in a decidedly more pleasant way than worrying about her gift shop or her ex.

With an imaginary shake of her head, she focused back on the man at her counter. "Thank you for the compliment, Alex. But I'm sure you came here for more than my little shop of treasures. You're welcome to browse, of course."

"You're very astute. Yes, I have come here with a plan. A big one. I want to turn this town into a destination spot. A place people will come to in droves, year-round."

Droves. People. Tourists. Shoppers. Money. Dana shoved the receipts she'd been going through into a drawer. The envelope from the attorney went with them. Money. She could use that kind of money. Hell, she could use any kind of money.

"You've definitely piqued my curiosity. How would you turn Willow Bay into a destination?"

"By building a resort like you've never seen before."

A resort? Here? "Where?" She glanced at Josh. "Does the town know?"

"Very close to here. In fact, I've—"

Josh interrupted. "There are a lot of details to go over before we can discuss specifics," he said, stuffing his hands deep in his pockets. "I'm just hearing about this today, and I haven't seen the plans yet. It's only a concept at this stage."

"Oh, it's way more than a concept."

"I'd be interested in seeing what you've pulled together," Dana said, trying not to tug at the thread of hope that had just shown up. The one that might help her solve her financial dilemma.

"I'd love to show you. Say, over dinner?"

Josh stepped closer. "As mayor, I should see those plans first."

"I think you're completely right on that, Josh," Dana said, not wanting to undermine him. Still, she couldn't contain her enthusiasm for anything that would bring money into Willow Bay. And Tangerine Treasures.

"Great," Alex said. "I'll bring the plans over to your office for you to review."

"Why don't we go get them now? I can go with you and

save you a trip."

Alex pulled his gaze away from Dana's. "All right."

Dana could have sworn Josh let out a sigh, as if relieved. His shoulders relaxed and he actually started to smile. Right up until Alex's next words.

"You'll have all afternoon to review them, then Dana and I can go over them at dinner." He picked Dana's hand up again. "When do you close?"

"Umm, probably around five. Not much activity in this weather."

"Great. I'll pick you up at, say six? We can go to that pizza joint I saw down the street."

She didn't really want to go to dinner with the suave Alexander Granson, but she'd backed herself into a corner trying to make Josh jealous. She couldn't very well refuse without looking like an idiot to both men. So Dana nodded and blocked Josh's tight lips from her peripheral vision by turning more toward Alex, trying very hard to dig up some enthusiasm for this dinner. "I'll meet you there."

"It's a date." Alex kissed the top of her hand again and headed for the door.

Josh stepped closer to Dana. Opened his mouth, closed it, then opened it again. Dana silently begged him to tell her not to go. But only silence filled the tension between them.

"Come on, mayor. Time's a-wasting," Alex said from the door.

With a snap, Josh's mouth closed, the sadness in his eyes a testament to something he just couldn't seem to say. Dana wanted to hug the sadness out of him, but part of her resented his silence. The man's shyness drove her crazy. Never opposed to taking the first step and asking someone out, her ex had shaken her confidence in that respect. She didn't trust her intuition very much anymore. Between that and her dire financial status, seeing Josh as more than a friend would have to wait.

"Have a good day, mayor." Dana opened the drawer and pulled out the receipts she'd been inputting into her spreadsheet.

Josh stood there for another long moment, then walked away. Dana didn't dare look up or she'd ask him to stay. Or come back when he was finished with Alex. But she couldn't. She'd done that with Jett, taken the first step, and look where that had gotten her. Two hundred thousand dollars in debt.

The bell on her closing door tinkled before she found the courage to look around her once again empty gift shop. Bereft like she'd never been before, the weight of her misery bowed Dana's shoulders. She had a mountain of debt she couldn't pay, a guy that didn't seem to know how to make a move, and a date with someone way too close to Jett's personality for her to be comfortable with.

This day was getting worse with each passing hour.

Chapter Four

Josh threw the rolled-up plans on his desk and tore off his raincoat, running his hands through soaked hair and shivering when cold drips fell beneath the collar of his shirt. He should have pulled his hood up. He should have taken Granson up on his offer to drive him the two blocks to his office.

He should have told Dana not to go out with the man.

Once again, he'd remained silent. Damn it. What the hell was it about Dana Ricci that turned him into a mute idiot? As soon as he asked the question, he knew the answer. He wasn't sure he'd measure up.

Dana had a zest for life she embraced with those soulful, deep brown eyes of hers that sparkled when she was happy. And the way her long ponytail swung back and forth as she told him something that had happened that day, her excitement visible in the loveliest of smiles and those two irresistible dimples.

With her Italian heritage, Dana's hands were just as much a part of a conversation with her as her voice. He loved her animation. Her joy in life. Her body. A bit thin, maybe, but perfect curves where they should be. Curves he wanted to run his hands over. He'd never even touched her skin, though he knew it would be as soft as he imagined.

Josh hung his raincoat to dry and sank into his office chair. He should tell Dana how he felt. Just put it out there and let her decide. She either wanted to give them a try or she didn't. Except, if she didn't, he'd lose the most precious thing he'd found in Willow Bay. Her friendship. They'd had more conversations than he could count about the town, life, even how to help Gladys. All superficial, though. Anything he knew about her, he'd gleaned in bits and pieces. He'd never asked her one personal thing. Getting personal meant opening up. Opening up meant taking the chance he'd get hurt again. And Sandra had done a damn good job of showing him how that felt.

I need excitement in my life, not boredom, Josh. I need more than you can provide.

Boring. She'd called him boring and he'd come to believe her. Now Dana had a dinner date with Alexander Granson and Josh's heart was stuck in limbo.

He fingered the plans. Granson was too slick, too polished. Josh didn't like him. But was that reason enough to hate his plans? The logic that had directed him toward his accounting career defied his first choice: burning the plans without looking at them. Instead, he tossed them into a nearby garbage can. Sitting back in his chair, he looked around his office at the off-white paint, at the pictures of Multnomah Falls near where he'd been raised. His diploma. The window blinds that needed dusting. Anywhere but at the garbage can.

After making a cup of coffee and cleaning the blinds, Josh sat and tried to focus on work. He needed to get Bernie's new projections done. His closest friend in Willow Bay had taken out a loan to upgrade her pizza shop, The Square Peg, and now was worried she'd miscalculated and would struggle to make ends meet. He stared at the figures on his screen, tried to extrapolate where she'd be by the end of the year if revenue held.

Nothing made sense. An itch at the back of his head, like someone staring at him, made it impossible to concentrate. Damn it. After trying three times, Josh slapped his hands on the desk and glared at the garbage can. He yanked the papers out, rolled the rubber bands off, and spread them out to take a look, his eyes widening.

This wasn't a simple resort. It was a small city. Josh stared at the overview. Granson hadn't been bragging when he said it would cover every bit of two hundred acres. Not a small hotel like he'd said, but fifteen stories, with wings for families and for adults. An indoor water park on the family side and what appeared to be bars on the other. Three restaurants. Outside, another water park with a family pool, plus a huge area with carnival rides that put state fairs to shame. Then, on the back side of the hotel, an adults-only pool with its own bar. Surrounding it all, back among the trees, walking paths lined with shops and cabins for those who wanted privacy. A self-contained village. Hell, it even had its own grocery store and medical clinic.

Granson's plan wouldn't help Willow Bay. It would completely take it over and bury it. There would be no reason to leave the resort to eat at Connie's cafe, to browse Dana's gift shop, or even enjoy nature's beauty with a walk on the beach. One of the plan pages showed a wall-sized screen with a live view of the beach and ocean.

Where was the small casino Granson had mentioned? Josh looked through the plans again and couldn't find it. Based on the page numbering, a couple pages were missing. The man was withholding information, Josh was certain of it. Even so, this place was huge. How could this possibly be good for Willow Bay? Everything outside of the resort would become a tourist ghost town.

Josh slowly rolled up the plans. He had a Dana-sized beef with Alexander Granson and couldn't let that affect decisions he made about the town. People were hurting and they needed money. Would that make it hard for them to see the long view here? Would they listen to reason?

Still holding the plans in his hand, Josh got up and looked out at the streaming rain. Not a single car drove past. It was as if Willow Bay was frozen in a snow-globe, only with rain. Something was needed to jar them out of this lack-of-money muck. He tapped his leg with the rolled papers. He'd always trusted this town and its people and it was time to trust them now. They'd have a town meeting, a group discussion of the pros and cons.

With that settled, he set the plans aside and sat down at his computer. A few hours later, he'd figured out Bernie's projections, plus he had a working flyer ready to email to everyone about the Grand Granson Plan and a pros and cons list for discussion. He stretched and glanced out the window, surprised to see it had grown dark. When his stomach growled, he printed out a copy of the flyer and discussion points, shut everything down, and shrugged into his slicker. Pulling the hood up, he locked the office and headed out to get some dinner.

~~~

Dana pulled into the parking lot at The Square Peg and turned her engine off, still unsure if she even wanted to go inside. Why had she ever agreed to meet Alex Granson for dinner? She needed to be home, trying to figure out how to get herself out of the mess Jett had created for her. Correction. She'd created. If she'd only filed those papers...

Never one to shirk on a promise, Dana pulled her hood up and waded through the downpour to go inside. She'd loved this place since the first time she'd seen it, with all the antique equipment and posters and license plates everywhere. And the pizza was to die for.

"Hi, Dana," the owner said as she passed by with an armful of pizza.

"Hi, Bernie."

"Grab a table anywhere." Bernie looked back over a mound of curly auburn hair.

"Actually, I'm here to meet— Oh, I see him now."

Bernie stopped, her eyes widening. "You're with the suit?"

Dana shrugged.

"But I thought—"

"Thought what?"

"Oh, nothing. Nothing at all." Bernie waved airily with her free hand. "Go on ahead. I'll come get your orders after I settle the Johnson twins down with some pizza."

Betty and Mike Johnson owned the hardware store. Their boys, three last month, were currently racing around the tables, expanding their territory as they went. They reached Alex's table, and Dana saw him scowling as they screamed past. Their harried mother corralled them and, with a firm hand, pulled them back to their own table.

Alex saw Dana and his frown upended. He got up as she walked to the table, helped her out of the wet slicker and hung it on the peg next to his coat. Dana smiled and slipped into the booth, almost sighing with relief when Alex sat opposite her instead of beside her. That kind of closeness she neither needed nor wanted.

"I'm glad you made it," Alex said, raising his voice to be heard over the ruckus the twins were making. He scowled at the other table.

Dana laughed. "Don't worry. The boys will settle down as soon as the pizza cools. They always do. Ah, there, see? They have already."

"Someone should teach those children a little

discipline."

"Said a man whom I'm guessing hasn't spent much time around children."

"I haven't, though I'm aware they can behave better in public."

"Some can." Dana nodded, turning back from watching the frazzled parents cutting up pizza and filling sippy cups. "No nieces or nephews?"

"No siblings."

"Ah, I'm sorry."

"No need to be sorry. I've had a good life."

"I'm sure you have. And sisters and brothers can be a real pain sometimes." Like when her sister, Cheryl, tried to talk her out of marrying Jett, advice she didn't want to hear at the time. Who knew she'd be right? Dana sure hadn't realized Jett was such an ass. Cheryl had tried to set her straight, but she'd chosen not to listen.

"It's also nice to know they love you even when you make mistakes."

"I don't make mistakes."

Dana took a sip of her water to keep from laughing. Everyone made mistakes. Everyone. The New York attorney's letter in her pocket was clear evidence of that.

"Well, none I can't fix myself, that is."

His smile really was disarming. All those white teeth in a perfect row. "You look perfect."

His smile widened. "Thank you."

Had she said that out loud? Lordy, she had. When would she learn to stop vocalizing thoughts? That honesty, directed toward Jett's lavish ways, had been one of the final straws that broke her marriage.

"You look troubled," Alex said.

"I'm fine."

Alex reached over and tapped the wrinkles between her

eyes, then covered her hand with his. "I feel like I already know you, Dana. You're special. Don't worry. You can tell me anything."

Dana had no idea how to respond to that. She barely knew this man and wasn't about to divulge interesting tidbits about her life.

"What can I get you?"

Oh, thank God. Bernie's timing was spectacularly on target, though the scowl on her face made no sense. Dana pulled her hand out from beneath her date's. "Have you looked at the menu, Alex?"

"Yes." He tapped the table. "No pasta?"

"We're a pizza parlor," Bernie said.

"Right. Well, if you'll permit me to order for you, Dana?" He arched an eyebrow.

Really? "Sorry, Alex. I know this restaurant better than you do." Dana turned to Bernie. "The usual for me."

"Got it."

"The usual?" Alex asked.

"I don't indulge in Bernie's amazing pizzas often, so when I do, I go all out."

"She does. Her pizza is piled high," Bernie said with a laugh.

"And could I have a Caesar salad? And a glass of red wine, please." If she was going to pig out, she planned to do it in style.

"You bet. And for you, Sir?" Bernie turned to Alex.

"I'll have a Caesar salad as well."

"Anything else?"

"No, that will be enough." Alex looked around. "Is there a wine list?"

Both women laughed heartily.

"Red or white. That's your list," Dana said.

Alex actually paled, so Dana let him off the hook,

leaning forward. "It's a well-kept secret that Bernie's red is a blend from a local winery. It's really quite good. The white, I'm not going to vouch for. My Italian blood doesn't do white."

"Red it is, then." He looked skeptical but held his opinion.

After Bernie went to start their orders, Alex leaned toward Dana. "Italian, eh?"

"Through and through. My grandparents emigrated here from the Milan area."

"The fashion capital of the world."

"I wouldn't know. I've never been."

"That's a shame, to not see your family's beautiful birthplace. I'd love to take you there someday, to show you the city I got to know."

"You lived there?"

"I apprenticed there for a summer. Thought I was going to go into fashion." He smoothed imaginary wrinkles out of his perfect white button-down shirt.

"What made you change careers?"

Alex shrugged. "It takes years to get noticed. I wanted to climb the ladder faster. Get to the top sooner. And I have."

Bernie delivered their wine and Alex took a sip of his. "Consider me impressed. This town surprises me every time I turn around. Good wine, beautiful women." He tipped his glass toward her.

Taking a sip of her own wine, Dana mused that she still hadn't figured out this man. He seemed like an opportunist, but he'd shown a kinder, gentler side when he noticed her frown earlier. Alex Granson was an enigma.

"So, what is it that you have planned for Willow Bay?"

He looked around the restaurant, taking in the paraphernalia on the walls. Antiques, mostly, with a few modern posters for effect. Dana knew them well. She'd been coming here ever since she'd moved to Willow Bay. It was a well-known local's hangout.

"I'm going to bring Willow Bay into the twenty-first century," Alex said.

"How?" Dana was nothing if not blunt.

"By creating a world that will draw people in. Make them want to be here no matter the time of year or the weather. Make them want to spend money."

"Again, how?"

"Well, your mayor still has the plans, but, in a nutshell, I'm going to build a resort like no one's ever seen before."

A resort? Dana had trouble picturing any kind of resort here. Something big could ruin Willow Bay's character. Dana didn't like the idea much. However, moves like this had put various places on the map. A resort would bring in people and people would shop. And shoppers meant a better bottom line for her. Maybe a chance to work on that newfound debt. Maybe she wouldn't lose Tangerine Treasures. Maybe, just maybe, this was the break she'd been looking for.

"Tell me more," she said, leaning her elbows on the table and giving Alex her undivided attention.

Chapter Five

Josh walked into The Square Peg deep in thought, so he didn't immediately see Dana and Granson in the far corner booth. When he did, he stopped dead in his tracks. Dana was leaning forward, *toward* Granson. *Toward him.* And her hands were moving, those long, animated fingers adding emphasis. Whatever conversation they were having, it was lively.

"Better close that mouth, my friend," Bernie said from behind the counter. "If Dana sees that, she'll figure out how you feel about her."

"Damn it, Bernie. Shut up."

Bernie chuckled as Josh joined her. "You really ought to just tell her. Take your chances."

"She's seemed so down lately."

"You never think it's the right time," Bernie set a glass of amber liquid in front of Josh. "Try this."

"The new brew?"

"Yes. I think I've finally got my first serious microbrew recipe," Bernie said as she pulled a pizza out of the oven and sliced it. "Be right back."

He sipped the beer, appreciating the bite, followed by a smooth, soothing taste. Bernie was right. This was her best concoction yet.

She delivered the pizza to Dana and Granson's table. Dana looked up, smiling. Josh knew the exact moment she noticed him. Her smile disappeared quicker than a gull once the French fries stopped flying.

"Yeah, she feels the same way I do. Right," Josh mumbled under his breath.

"You never know until you try." Bernie stepped back behind the counter.

"Bernie, you're just about the best friend I've got here. You vouched for me when I first came to town. So I know you're smart."

"Yeah, yeah."

"So how come, when a woman is out with another man and gives me the evil eye when she sees me, you think she likes me."

Bernie leaned her elbows on the counter and put her hand in front of Josh's face. "One,"—she counted on her fingers—" I see the way she looks at you when you're not looking. Two,"—another finger shot up—" she's never looked at another guy that way since I've known her, and three,"—that finger shot up—" she's probably on a date with another guy because you won't ask her out."

She kept her fingers there until Josh grabbed them. He glanced at Dana, still frowning his way.

"Come on," Bernie said. "Help me clear the Johnson table and tell me how much you love my new beer. Your dinner is almost ready."

Josh's authentic compliments about the beer widened Bernie's smile as they piled dishes on the pizza trays and carried them back to the kitchen. Josh leaned against the counter while Bernie hosed them off and put them in the washer.

"How come you and I never hit it off like those two out there?"

"First— Damn, I'm counting again. Okay, look." Bernie dried her hands and grabbed Josh's shoulders. "We'd kill each other if we tried to be a couple, Josh. We're much better friends. By the way, I don't get the impression those two are hitting it off that well."

"You don't?"

"No, but if you don't make your move soon, someone else will, and your chance will be lost."

Bernie went to the oven, pulled an individual lasagna out, and wrapped it to go for Josh. "Don't let the suit know I made this for you. He wanted pasta and that is so not on the menu for the masses. Only for special friends."

"Like me?" Josh grinned for the first time in what felt like days.

"Yes. Like you. Don't let it go to your head."

"Thanks, Bernie."

Something yipped behind him and Josh poked his head around the corner. Two small puppies huddled together in a cage.

"You find another couple strays?"

She nodded. "They were wandering along the side of the road. I'm taking them over to the rescue shelter once I close."

"That's my Bernie. Always helping strays." Josh laughed and pecked her cheek. "I think I'll head home and get some work done on the house."

"When are you going to let me see the place?"

"When I'm done renovating. I'm almost done with your revenue projections, by the way. I'll stop by tomorrow to discuss them." He waved and, with a last glance at the couple on the far side of the room who seemed deep in discussion, Josh left for home.

As he unlocked his front door, he noticed that the mansion next to his had the usual lights on. He had no idea if anyone even lived there. It was owned by some company. He'd checked. And he'd never seen anyone home. A caretaker kept the yard in shape and each morning, those lights were off. Maybe they were on a timer.

The instant he set his keys in the tray on the sideboard near his door, Josh relaxed. Home. The old mansion he'd been restoring since he'd bought it a year ago. Granted, with his day jobs, the renovation was a slow process. Most of the main rooms were still studs, but the electrical and plumbing were done and he had heat. Thank goodness.

Setting his dinner on a TV tray, the lone table in the front room, he went to the fridge and grabbed a beer. His favorite cushy leather recliner waited for him, the only other piece of furniture in the room save for his TV and stand. He flicked on the television to the news while he ate, taking time to send mental thanks out to Bernie as the Italian pasta slid past his taste buds. Never much of a cook, Josh could still appreciate what it took to make something this good.

So good, it almost made him forget Dana's date with Granson. Almost. Those two together had thrown Josh completely off-kilter. The man hadn't seemed her type at all. She was small town, Granson was big city. Except... Josh's fork stopped midway to his mouth. Was that true? Was she small town?

"Oh, my God," he said to the wall. "I don't even know where she's from."

How could that be? All this time he'd wanted her, loved her laugh, her enthusiasm, her expressive hands, and he didn't know where she'd been raised? Had he been so focused on what she wouldn't see in him that he'd never bothered to learn more about her?

Disgusted with himself and no longer hungry, Josh got up and put his dinner in the fridge. He'd always considered himself a man who cared about others, and his feelings for

Dana went way beyond that. Yet he didn't know this basic fact about her life. He was an idiot. A complete, certifiable idiot.

He picked up a hammer, thinking some good old-fashioned work might ease his frustration. Half an hour later, he was no better off.

A run. That's what he needed. Who cared if it was forty degrees and dark? These beaches were his backyard. He changed and headed out, hoping the night run would quell the remorseful beast inside him.

~~~

"I'd like to make sure you get home safe," Alex said as they stood beside her car.

"I have to get Duffy at the shop, and I need to finish a few things there." Hopefully, that would be enough to get him to go home. Alone. The more time she spent with him, the more she realized just how like Jett he was. At one point, she'd had to stop herself from calling him Jett.

"Oh. I thought—" He reached for Dana's hand, pulled it to his lips, and kissed it. "I thought we made a connection."

She tried really hard not to roll her eyes and decided to be blunt. "I don't put out on the first date, Alex."

He stepped back to stare at her, then laughed. "I love your honesty. Wow. And, well, you can't blame a man for trying, right?" He shrugged.

Dana laughed. Just when she thought she wanted nothing to do with Alexander Granson, he found a way around it. "No. I guess I can't blame you. But it's late and I have a long day tomorrow."

"It's barely eight."

"Carpets get rolled up pretty early here, especially in the winter." She opened her car door. "Thank you, Alex. I had a nice time tonight."

"Nice, huh? I'm going to have to do something to rise

above nice, I guess."

"Nice is fine by me. Good night."

Alex stood there as she pulled away. Dana couldn't help the deep breath of air she took as she left. There was something about the man she just didn't trust.

Back at the shop, Dana let herself in, locked up, and walked through the store, no lights necessary, she knew it so well. She smiled when she heard scratching at the door to her private quarters. When she opened it, Duffy bounded out, bouncing around her legs and jumping up, then down, up, then down.

"Stop it," Dana said, laughing. She dropped to the floor to let him lick her face. She hugged him tight. "You love me no matter what, don't you, boy?"

He wiggled in her lap.

"Need to go for a walk?"

The wiggling got more enthusiastic.

"All right. Let me change my clothes and put on my winter gear and we'll get you your outdoor time."

Five minutes later, she was bundled up, had pulled on her rubber boots, and Duffy had his harness on. Dana locked the back door behind her. Rounding the corner toward the beach, she gasped as the wind hit her. Not a strong wind, but it didn't take much of a chill factor to make it feel like they were at the freezing mark. Brrr. Thank goodness it had stopped raining.

"Come on, boy. Let's get this over with. It's cold out."

They headed out over the dunes to the beach, Duffy's favorite playground no matter the weather. The moon, close to full, shed enough light for their walk through the soft sand. Once on the beach, she took Duffy's leash off and let him run. And run he did, stopping here and there to sniff and leave his scent, then run off again.

Dana followed more slowly, thinking about her day.

And night. Alex Granson was a very handsome man, and his attention, while flattering, held too many Jett-echoes. What little she knew of his plans seemed larger than life. Could Willow Bay sustain a project like that? The biggest carrot he'd dangled had been the financial gain shops like hers would see with an influx of vacationers. That was a very big carrot, and Dana couldn't figure out why she was holding back her support of the project.

A lone runner raced along the waterline, dodging tide pools here and there.

Alex said he'd given Josh more specific information. Maybe she could get Josh to show it to her, to get a better idea of the master plan.

Duffy tore off after the runner, barking and yipping.

Oh, no. Dana raced after him, yelling for him to stop and come back to her. She really should invest in those obedience lessons.

The runner stopped. Duffy chased around in circles, then leaped up into the person's arms.

"Duffy!" Dana hollered. "Stop that!"

"It's okay," a male voice said as she drew closer. A voice she knew.

"Oh, Josh. It's you. I wondered why Duffy took off like that."

Josh smiled as he scratched the dog's ears, then set him down. Appropriately petted, Duffy returned to his examination of the seaside smells.

"Why are you out—" they both spoke at the same time, then laughed.

"Sorry, you first," Josh said.

"Why are you out running at night?" Dana said.

"Just needed to clear my head," he answered hastily. "You?"

"Duffy needed his evening walk."

"Ah, yes, you were busy earlier."

Dana hoped darkness hid the blush she felt creeping up her cheeks. "I—" She didn't normally wait for someone else to pick up the ball. She preferred being forthright and honest. And she wanted Josh to like her. She'd taken the bull by the horns with Jett and look where that had gotten her. Dana refused to go that route again. She was going to take the traditional route, even if it killed her heart.

"Yes," she finally said. "I was out with Alex."

Josh stiffened. "Did you have a good time?"

"He's an...interesting man."

With unspoken accord, they started walking back toward the path into town.

"Looks like the date ended pretty early."

Josh sounded way too pleased by that thought. "How do you know he's not back at my place waiting for me while I take Duffy out?"

Josh stumbled and almost fell. "Is he?"

"I think that's way beyond the purview of a friend to ask." Okay, that sounded pretty grumpy, even to her. Dana realized Josh had stopped walking. She turned back to him.

"Is he waiting for you?" he asked again, his voice a deeper, more gravelly version of its normal self. Was he jealous? Dana's heart lightened just a bit at that thought. But, since she also wasn't one to play games, she let him off the hook. "No."

"Good."

"Why?"

Josh stepped closer to her. With only the moon for light, his face was in shadow beneath his hood, and Dana couldn't see his expression. There wasn't much need, though, since he didn't stop. He pulled her into his arms, his lips crushing hers with the intensity of his kiss. Dana gave herself over to the exquisite feel of his lips on hers, demanding, begging, so unlike the Josh she knew. The scent of the sea swirled around them as he deepened the kiss, coaxing her mouth open.

She did so willingly, wanting more, needing more. There was no cold, no wind. Only Josh.

When he broke the kiss, he held her neck and leaned his forehead against hers as both of them caught their breath. Finally, after long moments, he pulled back his hood so she could see the passion flaming in his eyes.

"That's why," he said, then turned and ran off down the beach.

Dana stared after him until he was lost to her sight. *What the hell was that?*

She called for Duffy, who came running up full of wet sand and fun memories. She walked back to her store in a daze. She cleaned up Duffy, who then curled up on his bed and went straight to sleep.

Dana wasn't sure what had happened with Josh out there on the beach. But two things she did know.

She wouldn't sleep much tonight.

Because she wanted more.

Chapter Six

Josh picked up the sheetrock and tried to set it in place to screw, but it didn't fit. What the hell? He'd measured it. Fighting the desire to throw the board, he laid it back on the table and paced the room a couple times to settle himself. Then he re-measured the space and the board, finding them off by an inch.

"Damn it."

He'd been working on the parlor walls since four a.m., unable to sleep. It should have calmed him down. Instead, he'd measured wrong three times already. At this rate, the renovation would cost him twice as much to finish.

"I shouldn't have kissed her. Not like that," he said to no one. That wasn't how he'd planned to make his intentions known. Dana was precious and deserved the gentle caress of someone in for the long haul. He'd been so strung out over that date of hers he'd acted on instinct, and probably ruined any chance he had. Damn it all to hell!

Still, that kiss! He'd wanted to taste her lips for so long, he'd been afraid the actual act wouldn't live up to his imagination. How wrong could he have been? Dana was an amazing woman and that kiss had been a hot, driving need shared between them.

Josh dropped the measuring tape. *Both. Of. Them.*

She'd returned his kiss. Maybe she felt at least a little of what he felt for her.

He needed a shower so he could get to town. To see Dana, talk to her.

Tell her he was in love with her.

He raced toward the shower, shedding clothes as he went. He needed to get to Dana now. Except...

Josh looked at his phone. It was seven a.m. Tangerine Treasures didn't open until ten a.m. And he didn't know where Dana lived. That was the one thing Dana had kept a closely guarded secret. He had no idea why. What was it about where she lived that she didn't want him to know?

He'd been afraid to pry. He soaked up every piece of information Dana imparted, but every time he'd gotten close to something personal, either he backed off or she side-stepped around it.

He showered, intent on going into the office. Might as well get some work done while he waited.

For ten a.m.

And the rest of his life to begin.

~~~

Dana turned Tangerine's sign from closed to open and unlocked the door, still thinking about the kiss that had robbed her of most of her sleep. Man, Josh could kiss. Who knew the mild-mannered mayor had such a take-charge side of him? Dana kind of liked that. Okay, she liked it a lot.

"It was just a kiss," she told Duffy, who, after getting his outdoor time this morning, happily settled on his dog bed behind the cash register for a well-deserved nap. "Just a kiss," she muttered again, as she noticed Gladys a couple stores down, her trusty shopping cart filled to the brim.

"Gladys," she called out, opening the door. "It's cold out. Come in and get warm."

"Oh, thanks, dearie." Gladys pushed her sopping wet cart right into the store, dripping all over floors designed to handle saltwater and sand. Dana would clean it later.

"Have a seat," she told the elderly lady. "Let me get you a cup of cocoa."

When Gladys gave her the stink-eye, she laughed.

"Okay, coffee it is. Heavy on the *cream*, right?"

The old woman patted Dana's cheek. "I always knew I liked you best."

Still chuckling, Dana went back to her apartment and came out with two cups of coffee, one black, one not. Once she'd learned that their resident un-homed person liked a little Bailey's in her coffee, she'd kept a small stock on hand.

Gladys wrapped her hands around the steaming cup, sniffing appreciatively. "Thank you. Just what my old soul needs."

"What are you doing out on a day like this? You should stay at the shelter." Dana didn't have to look outside to know the rain had increased, as had the wind. She could hear the drops hitting her windows like ice pellets. She sighed. There would be no shoppers again today.

"Gotta keep my eye on this place."

"On my shop?" Dana pulled a chair over and sat across from Gladys.

"On the town."

Gladys, whose entire life seemed to be dripping wet in a shopping cart near the door, kept an eye on the town? "Why?"

Instead of answering, the old woman took a sip of her coffee, sighed, then stood. "This is some good coffee right here. I thank you for it."

"Leaving already? You've 'hardly dried off." Dana stood and put a lid on the to-go cup for her friend.

"I gotta keep moving. No time to stop."

"But it's cold and wet outside."

"Pah! This ain't nothing compared to the worst Mother Nature can send. This is just a little squall. I can handle it." She tugged at her bright yellow slicker. "I've got Lucy here to keep me dry."

Dana chuckled just as the bell above the door tinkled and Alex walked in. Great. She wasn't ready to deal with him this morning.

"Oh, hi," Dana said.

"Good morning," he said, looking askance at Gladys. "Are you busy? I thought you might help me with some advice on how to approach the townspeople about my" — he glanced again at Gladys— "ideas."

"Townspeople don't need no outsider giving them ideas," Gladys grumbled.

"It's not like they've come up with anything themselves," Alex retorted.

Gladys made fists with her hands and stepped toward Alex. "Don't you dare speak bad about Willow Bay."

Things were getting out of hand and Dana knew she was the one with the power to stop it. Setting her personal opinion about Alex aside, she stepped between him and Gladys, put a hand on his chest, and looked up, imploring him to be patient. He stared down at her for a long moment then, covering her hand with his, he nodded.

When he was like this, when he considered her feelings, he really was rather sweet.

Thank you, Dana mouthed. She turned back to Gladys as Alex moved off toward the counter." Can I give you a ride somewhere, Gladys? Help you stay dry?"

"A little bit of rain won't hurt me. I'm strong, like Willow Bay." She glared over Dana's shoulder at the man, then leaned forward. "Don't let fancy-pants sway you, dearie. Willow Bay don't need his kind."

"Alex has a plan to bring in more tourists. Would that be so bad? We could all use the money," Dana replied. Boy, could she use the money.

Gladys patted Dana's cheek again before pulling on her gloves. "I know some people are hurting. You too, I guess."

"And you, Gladys."

"Me? I'm fine. Living just the life I want to live. Just don't take what he says at face value. Promise me that."

Dana sighed. "Okay, Gladys. I promise." She helped the old woman get her cart back outside, shaking her head as she watched her trudge off into the rain. Dana grabbed some rags to soak up the rainwater that had dripped from Gladys' cart onto the floor. Alex sat in one of the vacated chairs.

"So, do you let the homeless people of this town make decisions for you?" he asked.

Dana laughed, refusing to be bated. "Gladys is a fixture here. She's been here since long before I arrived. We all keep an eye on her and help when she lets us."

~~~

Josh backed away from the window as Dana cleaned up the water on the floor. Gladys glared at him as she pushed her cart past, mumbling under her breath. He leaned against the building, trying to calm his nerves.

To see Dana's hand resting on Granson's chest as she gazed up at him with such a vulnerable look on her face about tore Josh's heart out. What had happened to change things between last night and this morning? She should be looking at *him* that way, not Granson.

He hung his head. She'd turned to someone else and it was his own fault. He'd waited too long.

Chapter Seven

"I can't believe you never filed for divorce, Dana," Aimi said.

Dana wanted to pound her cell phone into the counter, but she couldn't afford to replace it. "Well, I didn't. I waited because I didn't know where Jett was and I wanted to tell him before I filed. I—I thought I owed him that."

"You don't owe him anything. That man drove your finances into the ground before you left him. Now, he's buried you even deeper."

"Like I don't already know that. I don't need you to rehash the facts, Aimi. I screwed up, not filing for the divorce. I. Know. That. But I need help and you're my best friend. I need you to tell me what to do. Please."

Aimi sighed, deep and long, and Dana knew she'd switched into attorney mode. "Okay, first off, sign those divorce papers and send them to me. I'll get them filed. We can't serve him because we don't know where he is, so we'll have to publish notices of your intent to divorce, but I'll put them in obscure legal papers. If Jett has come back to Spokane, which I very much doubt, he'll never see them."

"Doesn't he have a right to know?" Dana chewed her bottom lip.

Another sigh. "Always trying to make sure everyone's happy. That's one of the things I love about you. But you need to understand, Jett moved to New York and had no problem piling up debt in your name. That's why the lawyers came after you. He knew what he was doing and he didn't care. So I want you to repeat after me, I don't owe Jett diddly-squat."

"I know, but—"

"No buts. Say the words."

"I—"

"Say. The. Words."

"All right. All right." Dana put her head in her free hand. Aimi was right, she really was. Still, this went against everything Dana had been taught. You took care of people. That's how she'd been raised.

She straightened. What was she thinking? Jett had totally screwed her over.

"I don't owe Jett diddly-squat."

"Now say it again, like you mean it."

"I don't owe Jett diddly-squat." She didn't. She really didn't. Dana raised her voice, strengthened it. "I don't owe Jett diddly-squat."

"Good. Now anytime you feel yourself wavering, you repeat that over and over until you remember you don't have to be nice to this man. And send me those divorce papers. Today."

Dana had put off visiting other shop owners with Alex until later in the afternoon. She could swing by the post office while they were out and about. "I'll send them."

"Good. You also need to give me the number of the attorneys in New York. Let me call them and threaten court if they push you too hard."

"Court?" Dana could see the Willow Bay gossip-mongers having a field day if she went to court over financial matters. "I don't want to go to court, Aimi."

"These things rarely get that far, but those attorneys need to know we can play hardball just as well as they can. And that I'm the person for them to contact, not you. Don't worry. We'll figure this out. But, just in case, pull together your finances."

"In case what?"

"Let's not go there until we have to."

Bankruptcy. That's what she meant. Dana sank into the chair next to Duffy's bed, sucking in deep breaths.

"It's okay, Dana. Really. We'll get this figured out."

"I'm so grateful for you. I know I'm asking a lot."

"Hey, you held me together when things at the office got so bad. How many nights did I drink all your wine and talk your ear off? This is peanuts compared to that."

"Well, still, I owe you."

"Not one dime. Well, maybe a girl's vacation when we resolve this."

"You're on."

Dana set her phone down and looked outside at the gray day. The rain had stopped and rumor had it the sun might actually make an appearance over the next couple of days. Even though Aimi had reassured her, Dana sent a prayer skyward for some money-spending tourists. She needed all the help she could get.

~~~

"So you see, I think you'll be fine as long as you don't overspend or have some expensive issue crop up in the next year." Josh closed the report he'd prepared for Bernie and pushed it across the booth to her.

"Thanks, Josh. I appreciate you doing that. I especially love the budget you worked out for me."

He laughed. "You are a sick person, Bern. Most people don't care for budgets."

"It helps. Now I can compare my monthly receipts—"

"You mean I can compare your monthly receipts."

"Well, yes, there is that." She reached over and patted his hand. "It's nice to know I'm not sinking in quicksand."

"You're the most popular eating joint in town, especially for us locals. You'll never sink. You just need to be careful after that kitchen upgrade."

"I can do that. You know I can."

"Yes, I do."

"So, now that the business is done, how are things with Dana going?"

Working hard not to cringe, Josh stared at Bernie, straight-faced.

"Don't try that blank expression with me," Bernie said. "I know you, remember? You like her a lot."

He shrugged, still not able to find his voice. This morning...

"I think she's made a choice."

"What? Did you finally talk to her?"

"No. But I saw her with Granson. In her store. They were...intimate."

"Seriously? In the store where anyone can see?"

"Not that kind of intimate." Though even the idea made his blood boil. "They were close. Touching. Like people who liked each other." He looked at Bernie. "I never thought she'd take to a city-slicker."

"I don't think she does, Josh."

"You didn't see them."

"No, I didn't. But something I overheard when they were here last night made me wonder if she's in trouble financially. She perked right up when he started talking about what his plans could do for the area."

Was Dana having more than the usual seasonal money trouble? Sure, she was a little disorganized, but he'd seen her working with her receipts, and during the season Tangerine Treasures did good business. If she needed help, why hadn't she asked him? This is what he did for a living, helped people figure these things out. Did she think so little of him? "She didn't ask me for help. I guess that tells you what she thinks of me."

Bernie laughed. "I think it says a lot about how she feels about you. She's got pride, Josh. A lot of it. She's not going to ask a man she likes to help dig her out of a hole."

"But that's what I do. That's my freaking job." He shoved the rest of his papers into his briefcase and got up.

Bernie stood and hugged him. "Give her time. Let her work through whatever's going on, then tell her how you feel. Or, just ask her out on a date. You have to make the first move."

He had, last night on the beach. She's kissed him back, too. And today, she'd gazed up at Granson, her hands on his chest. Maybe it was time to put this fantasy to bed. Damn. Wrong analogy. Or maybe it was time for him to fight back. Except, if he wasn't Dana's choice, her happiness was more important than his heart. Torn between what he wanted and Dana's right to choose, Josh didn't know what to do. For now, he needed time to think.

"So, when are you going to start dating?" Josh tried to turn the tables on Bernie. "You've had, what, three dates in the five years I've been here?"

"No one in town lights my fire and you know that. Nice deflection, my friend, but it's not going to work. Tell Dana how you feel, and soon. Before you lose her."

How could he lose someone he never had?

Driving back to the office, Josh couldn't resist taking the ocean road and swinging by the gift shop. He frowned at the closed sign. Dana rarely closed during the day, weekday or weekend. He pulled in, got out, and peered in the window.

The lights were off and he couldn't see Duffy, but everything else looked normal.

"Where is she?" He looked up and down the strip. Nothing was open so Josh got back in his car and headed for the office. He finalized a couple of jobs then called it a day around four so he could stop at the grocery store on his way home.

Josh walked into Sam's Grocery and stopped short. Dana stood at the register talking to Sam and a couple other Willow Bay residents. Granson stood with his had at her back

"...could have far-reaching ramifications for Willow Bay," he said.

"We could all use more income, right?" Dana said.

What the hell?

Sam nodded, then noticed Josh and waved him over. "Hi, mayor."

With a light blush tinting her cheeks, Dana took a step back from Alex, glancing at Josh, then quickly away. Did she know how he felt about her? Or have maybe an inkling of feeling for him?

Granson, on the other hand, grinned and tried to put his arm around Dana's waist, which she side-stepped.

"There's our illustrious leader now," Granson said.

"What's going on?"

"We're just talking to folks about how my resort will put Willow Bay on the map and bring in a lot of tourists."

"Tourists, maybe. But will it bring customers?" Josh was pissed and not attempting to hide it. "And you agreed we'd set up a town meeting to discuss this with the entire community."

"Doesn't hurt to start drumming up opinions in advance. That's good business," Granson said.

Sam and the others watched with interest. Josh always

tried to be fair and he knew part of the reason he didn't like this resort idea was Granson's proprietary attitude toward Dana. Damn, that stuck a dagger right through his heart. Still, this resort just didn't seem to be the right fit for the people who lived here.

"As long as you're giving the pros and the cons."

"There are no cons," Granson said with a grin. "This is a win-win for everyone."

"Are we going to have a meeting?" Sam asked.

"Definitely," Josh answered. "In fact, let me grab a flyer. I've reserved the community hall for next Saturday. Be right back."

When he returned, Dana and Granson had separated by a few feet, which made breathing much easier for Josh. "Here you go, Sam. Anna. Julie. Take a few and pass them around."

Granson intercepted one of the flyers, frowning. "Saturday? Couldn't do it sooner?"

Josh held Granson's gaze with equal consternation. "We need time to get the word out. Besides, there's no hurry, right?"

Granson pursed his lips and drew in a deep breath, plastering a smile back on his face. "Not at all. And I'll be there to show Willow Bay just how good this will be for them." He reached for Dana's hand. "Besides, I'll have more time to get to know this beauty."

Shit. Josh gnashed his jaw, refusing to get drawn in. He looked at Dana, who seemed uncomfortable.

"Do you want a ride home?" Josh asked her, leaning in.

"I can take Dana home," Granson said.

"Maybe she doesn't want you to." He looked at Dana, silently pleaded with her to come with him.

"I'm okay, Josh. I came with Alex, so he can drop me off home," she said, chewing her lip.

Slap. The hand across his face hadn't been literal, but Josh had been slapped nonetheless. Had Granson completely won Dana? She looked so forlorn and uncomfortable, like she didn't want to hurt anyone. Him or Granson? Josh couldn't tell.

He needed to know she'd be okay. And sleeping alone. But he had no right to intrude into her life that way.

"Fair enough," Josh said to Dana. "My apologies. I shouldn't have put you in that position." He looked around at the group, which had grown. "If you'll excuse me, I'll finish my shopping and head for home. See you all on Saturday."

Josh wandered around the store throwing items in his cart, barely aware of the things he grabbed. He was an idiot. He should have scheduled that meeting for tomorrow, gotten Granson out of town sooner, and his claws out of Dana. Unable to delay any longer, Josh headed for the register, relieved to see Granson and Dana had left.

"You don't like that guy much, do you, mayor?" Sam asked while he scanned Josh's groceries.

Absolutely not. "It's not how I feel about him that matters. It's what's best for Willow Bay."

"That's why this town likes you, Josh. You think things through, and you're doing the right thing, letting the town give its opinion."

"I just hope the decision we make works for Willow Bay."

"I'll be at the meeting and I'll listen to this guy, but I get the impression you and I are on the same page. Sounds like a pretty grand plan for our little town."

"Grand is a good description." Josh said goodbye and got out of the store with his self-respect barely intact. Why had he let Granson goad him into that show of testosterone? He needed to get a handle on his temper.

He also needed to either tell Dana how he felt or let her go. His breath hitched at that last thought. No, that wasn't an option. Would she listen to him? He wasn't slick or interesting like Alexander Granson.

I need excitement in my life, not boredom.

Sandra's words flashed like a bad rerun through his brain. Over, and over, and over again. He was a small-town accountant. Granson was a big-city guy. Fashionable. Interesting. Josh worked, ate, and went home. That was his life. He was a small-town accountant. Granson was a big-city guy.

Josh pulled into his driveway and grabbed his groceries. As he let himself in, he realized there was one more thing he needed before he could even think about relaxing tonight. To know he hadn't completely alienated Dana. Tonight. Now.

Josh dialed Bernie.

"Square Peg. How can I help you?"

"Are Dana and Granson there having dinner?"

"Haven't seen them today. Why? You looking for Dana? Finally going to come clean?"

"I just—oh, never mind. I'll call her. Thanks." He hung up and put his groceries away. Sour cream? Why had he bought sour cream? And this wasn't his normal brand of beer. Grabbing one anyway, Josh dialed Tangerine Treasures.

"Hello?"

Relief rushed through him. "You're at the store."

"Josh? Yes, I'm at the store. Where else would I be?"

Out with the asshole. Or worse, at his hotel. "Nowhere. I just...I felt bad about how I left things at the market. I wanted to apologize again."

Dana chuckled. "Things did get a little tense."

"I never meant for you to be in the middle of that."

"I know you didn't."

Mention the kiss. Tell her it was an explosion of awesomeness.
"And, um, last night, on the beach..."

"You mean that kiss?"

"Yes." *That smoking-hot kiss that rocked my world.* "I should probably apologize for that, too."

"Not on my account."

"So you liked the kiss, then." Josh held his breath, waiting for the make-or-break moment.

"Yes, Josh, trust me when I say you are a very good kisser." Her breathy answer settled in his heart like a wave wrapping around his ankles, tickling his nerves into calmness. Until he remembered Alex at the grocery store.

"What's up with you and Granson? Are you an item?"

Dana took a long breath and let it out. "He seems to think so. I'm not— Well, I have a lot to think about."

If she was unsure, there was still a chance. Josh's heart lightened at the thought. "Anything I can do to help?"

"No, Josh. I'm sorry, but I have to figure this out myself."

She sounded tired. Was she talking about her and Granson or about her financial worries? "I'd like to help, Dana. If you ever need anything, all you have to do is call."

"Ah, Josh, you are so sweet. Right now, there are things I need to handle myself. I hope you can understand that."

Sweet? She thought he was sweet? He should march over there right now and show her how not sweet he wanted to be. Except that wasn't his way. Dana had the right to choose. Josh wanted to fix whatever was wrong in Dana's life, to give her a reason to smile. She had a right to deal with things in her own way and on her own timeline. He'd have to respect that, though Granson's involvement in her issues grated on him.

"You shouldn't trust Granson, Dana."

"At least he's got ideas."

Ouch. That hurt. "Have you seen his plans?"

"No. He says you have the only set he brought."

"I could bring them over. Now. Or later tonight, if you'd like to see them."

"I'm pretty tired. Maybe tomorrow?"

"That's fine. Come by the office any time and I'll show them to you. Or I can bring them by the shop. I think it's important to understand what he wants to build before you climb on his bandwagon."

The pause on the other end of the phone should have told him something, but Josh forged on ahead. "Granson's resort probably isn't a good fit for Willow Bay."

"Seems to me," Dana said with a flat voice, "anything that brings in money-spending tourists would be good for this town. I don't think you're giving the plan much of a chance."

Josh let his breath out slowly. "The place will be bigger than Disneyland. How can you think that fits here?"

"Because it will bring an influx of money. We need more tourists, Josh."

"Dana, are you struggling? I can take a look at things, help you figure out a plan to survive."

Too long of a pause happened before she answered.

"I'm fine."

Yeah, and that fierce, I'm-lying-through-my-teeth grate to her voice belied her words.

"Seriously. I can help."

"Seriously," Dana repeated. "I don't need help. I'm fine." Now her words were coming out staccato. She definitely needed help. Josh searched for a way to convince her.

"Look, I have to go," she said. "But Josh? Alex's plan just might help. Don't get mired in the ordinary or you'll do us all a disservice."

"Ordinary?" he said, picking up on the one word that could deflate him.

Dana hung up without answering. Josh stared at the cell phone that had reverted to its main screen. How had that conversation gone from good to bad so quickly? Shit. He'd called to apologize and had made things worse instead of better.

Damn it. She'd called him ordinary. And what was with her siding with Granson? Did she really believe this resort was a good fit for the town? Was she that much of a money-grubber that she'd go with any crazy idea?

With Sandra, money had driven every decision she'd made. Well, not every single one.

You're boring, Josh. I need excitement in my life.

Boring. No matter how many times he had blocked that word from his mind, it crept back in. Los Angeles moved in the fast lane and he didn't, so she'd left him for someone who sparked her interest more, who sped through life without taking time to savor the moment. It was always about the next rush, and that wasn't how Josh wanted to live his life so he'd left the condo and Sandra and moved to Willow Bay. Josh rarely looked back, except for times when those words pounded their way to the front of his brain.

Boring. Ordinary.

Boring.

Chapter Eight

The ocean's roar soothed Dana as she walked the beach while Duffy explored. She glanced at her watch. Another hour until she had to open the shop. She drew in a deep breath of the salty air, glad she'd come out early. The beach, the sand, the ocean waves that tried to steal her shoes—all these things relaxed her and remained among the primary reasons she loved Willow Bay. Dana turned her face up to the rare winter sunshine. It wouldn't be warm today, but the sun was welcome nonetheless.

Times like this, on the beach, always righted her world when it spun out of control. Two days had passed since her conversation with Josh and she couldn't stop thinking about it.

She'd baited him, again, and that wasn't her style. Josh was the sensible one, always thinking issues through and doing things right the first time. Dana was nothing but a screw-up. And when he'd started in on Alex's plan when the tourists it might bring were the only thing between Dana and living life on the street like Gladys, she'd taken Alex's side. So far, his plan was her only chance to get out of this hole. Dana hung her head. Would the town she'd come to love change because of this? She hoped not. She really needed to see those plans, but after how she and Josh had left things, she hadn't wanted to call him.

Dana stretched her arms above her head and let out a noisy yawn. Sleep had eluded her the night before not only because of Josh. Aimi had called.

"The good news is, I've filed your divorce papers and placed the notices."

Okay. A good start.

"However, the collection lawyer in New York is unwilling to budge. I threatened with every trick in my arsenal and he basically said 'bring it on.' With no legal basis, he's pressing for payments to start in the next couple weeks. He can't do that."

"But he is."

"He's trying. Don't you send him a single ceOnt. We'll get this resolved."

Dana pulled a half-buried shell out of the sand. Broken, just like her life. She didn't have any money to send this lawyer. Hell, she didn't even have something to hock to buy her some time. She was so screwed. Aimi had thrown her a lifeline, though.

"I've hired a private investigator to track Jett down," she'd said. "I'm going to find that scumball and make him pay."

Except, if he'd gone so far in debt and skipped out, he didn't have any funds, either.

The wind picked up as a cloud covered her slice of sunshine, causing Dana to shiver as the air chilled. "Duffy! Come on, time to go to work."

Back at the shop, she cleaned and fed Duffy, unlocked the door, and switched the sign to open. She didn't hold out hopes for many tourists, but even in winter, late-week days sometimes brought storm-watchers into town. And razor clam digging opened tomorrow. Maybe that would bring some people in for the weekend. She booted up her computer but didn't open her business spreadsheet. She couldn't stand to stare at all the red, red, red. Dana put her head in her hands. How was she going to dig out of this?

Several hours later, the door's rare jingle brought her head up, her heart filled with hope, but it wasn't a tourist. It was Josh, and she was so happy to see him. Right up until she remembered the fight they'd had. He brightened her day, except when they were at odds. She tapped her chest in the vicinity of her heart, willing it to not feel the pain.

"I have Granson's plans," Josh said, holding up the rolled papers. "I tried to give you some space, but you need to see how grand his idea is before you go plugging it around town anymore."

"Willow Bay needs help, Josh."

"Not this kind. We'll find something else."

"What?"

Josh raked his hands through his hair. "I don't know, Dana. I'm trying to figure something out, so if you have any ideas, I'm happy to hear them." He held up his hand. "Other than Granson's."

"Well, Alex is here and now, not some vague 'we'll think of something' down the road."

"Just how much trouble are you in that you've jumped right into his wagon?"

"Whether I'm in trouble or not is none of your business, Joshua Morgan. Stop trying to invade my personal life. I can take care of myself."

"Dana, I want to help."

She would love nothing more than to hand over her mess and let Josh clean it up, but she'd created it. She needed to clean it up. And honestly, how could she ever tell Josh how bad she'd let it get?

"I respect your opinion, Josh, but right now, we're at an

impass."

He stared at her for a long moment, then strode to the counter she stood behind. "Yeah. I think you're right." He set the plans on the counter and stomped to the door, then stopped. Striding back, he came right around the counter and reached for Dana's shoulders, cupping them gently. "Let me help. Whatever's going on, Dana, please let me help."

She almost buckled. Maybe hiring a financial planner was the smart way to go. It would be so easy to just fall into his arms, to let Josh figure out a way past all her problems. But he wouldn't consider something Dana thought had merit, that maybe Alex's plan was good for the town. Would Josh expect her to only consider his ideas for resolution? Would he listen to her? Dana stepped back, hugging herself, and said nothing.

After a moment, Josh dropped his hands and walked slowly out of the store. Dana clutched herself tight, afraid that if she let go she'd race after him, beg him to help.

No. This was her problem to solve, no one else's. But damn, she'd never felt so alone. She wanted to curl up and forget the world for a while. The off chance a customer would walk in and spend some money kept her glued to the counter, staring out into the world beyond her shop, praying for a solution. If this weren't a labor of love, it could get monotonous. Long days, weeks, months. Owning a business wasn't for the fainthearted.

Dana picked up rolled plans. Josh was right about one thing. She needed to understand Alex's ideas before she went any further with this. She'd jumped on the bandwagon without much information and it was time to change that. She'd just rolled the bands off the papers when the bell tinkled and a customer came in, so she tucked them underneath the counter. The plans would have to wait until later.

~~~

Josh strode to his office but didn't make it very far. Gladys waylaid him at the corner of the row of buildings.

"Mayor?"

"Not now, Gladys." Josh stomped past the woman and her cart, then stopped. With a long sigh, he turned back.

"Bad day?" Gladys asked.

"Bad week."

"Well, if you need a pick-me-up, you should try Connie's new chowder over at the diner." Gladys pointed across the street like Josh didn't know where it was. "It's amazing. She just won a contest in California!"

"That's great." He glanced back at the gift shop as he spoke. "I'll have to stop by and congratulate her. Later."

Gladys grabbed hold of Joshua's hand with surprising strength. "Feel this? This here's the flesh and blood of Willow Bay." She shook, taking his hand with her. "There's warmth and love and companionship here. This is what you need to believe in, mayor. The rest will all fall into place."

Josh extracted his hand. "I'm not so sure about that." He tried to upend his frown. "Do you need a ride anywhere? Something to eat? You doing okay?"

She waved her hand in the air. "Me? I'm fine. Right as rain. Oh, shouldn't have said that. It'll come back now. Always does."

Josh nodded, said goodbye, and went to his office. He'd lost his temper with Dana. Barely acknowledged Gladys or her chowder story, and needed a punching bag to work through all his angry adrenalin. Screw it.

He locked the office and headed out. Half an hour later, he was pounding nails. He should be sheet-rocking, but that took a delicate hand and he was far from delicate at the moment so he went upstairs and re-framed a doorway instead. The house had five bedrooms over three floors.

He'd taken two of them on the second floor and turned them into one large master. Still bare bones, but the plumbing was in for the bathroom. If he could get this framed in, he was ready for insulation on the outer walls and sheetrock all around here.

Pound. Pound. Pound. He'd probably get this renovation complete about the time that resort of Granson's went live and turned Willow Bay into a circus. Ugh. Josh couldn't stand it. Was he ready for the town meeting tomorrow night? Unsure, he went downstairs and grabbed the pros and cons list he'd done up. He thought about his opening remarks as he went back to pounding nails. He thought about looking out into the crowd, seeing Dana.

Dana, who'd picked her side and maybe her man. Dana, who needed money for reasons she'd chosen to keep from him. Had she told Granson?

He had a hard time seeing Dana as a gold-digger like his ex, but it seemed like every time they fought, it was about money. And Granson was all about the money. Josh was certain of that.

God, could he have been that wrong about Dana?

He wished Dana could come up with something award-winning like Connie's chowder, or Bernie's beer. Maybe then she'd have money.

Josh froze, his hammer mid-swing. Money. Chowder. Willow Bay. Could it be that simple? He looked at his watch. Oh, man, he didn't have much time. Tossing the hammer, he raced downstairs, snatched up his keys and coat, and ran out the door. He needed to be at the office. He had a lot of research to do between now and the town meeting on Saturday, but by God, if he could pull this off, he'd have an alternative to Granson's grandiose plan.

Chapter Nine

Friday morning, Dana flipped the open sign at 10a.m. sharp and was surprised to see a couple standing outside with what looked to be their teenage daughter.

"Hi," she said as they entered the store.

"Hi," the teenager said, pulling off her knit hat and letting her blonde ponytail swing from side to side.

"Hello," the father said. "Do you happen to carry any clam digging supplies?"

Patting herself on the back for having stocked them just last month, Dana smiled and pointed toward the display.

"Thank you," the mother said. She leaned closer and lowered her voice. "We had to drag her here and there was no way she was putting a shovel in the sand for some ugly creature. Two clams later, she was stealing my shovel, so we're getting her one of her own."

Dana laughed. "You're good parents."

The woman shook her head. "Smart parents would have packed a third shovel just in case." She looked at the one her husband held out. "Thankfully, you're not out to gouge us."

"I sell for just a bit over my cost."

"That's refreshing," she said as she paid for the shovel. Her husband stood by the door, ready to get back to the beach. "Is the ice cream parlor open this afternoon?"

"It's hit or miss, though with clam season opening, it should be."

"Great. We'll swing back by, then." She looked around. "Might have to browse a bit."

Their car pulled out of the parking lot and Dana was again alone with her thoughts. A nice start to the day, though. A very nice start.

By midafternoon, she'd had several more people in the store, all in the mood to buy things and give Duffy a quick pet, which he soaked up like a movie star. She'd seen folks going in and out of the Willow Bay Café across the street. Connie would be happy. Dana stepped outside with Duffy during a lull and noticed the ice cream shop was indeed open.

Today was definitely a good day. Except... She glanced down the street. She hadn't seen Josh all day. He almost always stopped by, even if only to say hi. She didn't like where they'd left things yesterday. He wanted to help, she knew that. But she couldn't tell him how deep her trouble was. He'd lose all respect for her. Josh's opinion of her had become more and more important the longer she'd lived there. He could help. She knew that. But Dana couldn't stand the idea of him thinking she was an idiot or a dupe.

"Another tough day?"

Dana turned to see Alex walking around his car, heading her way.

She shook her head, both in answer and to clear the cobwebs. "Actually, it's been a good day."

"Great. I was hoping I could convince you to close early. I heard there's a place in the next town that is supposed to serve the best pie around."

"Duffy's, right?"

"The dog?" Alex pointed. "He's right there with those kids."

"No. Duffy's is the name of the restaurant."

"You named your dog after an eatery?"

Dana laughed. "Happy circumstance only. Duffy's a rescue so he came with the name. It suited him, so I kept it."

"Ahh, that explains that. So," Alex took both her hands in his and kissed the tops of each. "What do you say? Want to play hooky and go out for a night on the town?"

Dana worked hard to keep from yanking her hands away. She disengaged as soon she politely could. "A night on the town around here means bed by 9 p.m."

Alex closed the distance between them. "I like that idea."

"I didn't mean—" Heat crawled up Dana's cheeks. Red-hot embarrassment. "I—" She couldn't find her voice.

He laughed and backed up. "I love it when you blush, dear Dana. Don't worry. I know you're not ready to take that step. Yet."

The smile diminished, replaced by an intensity she'd never seen from Alex before. It made Dana nervous. She should tell him the truth, that she's not interested. His plans for Willow Bay interested her more than the man himself.

"Alex—"

"I hope to convince you to take the chance one of these days. Just putting you on notice."

She held her hands to her flaming cheeks, trying to clear her head. "I don't think—"

"So, dinner tonight?"

Dana couldn't help herself. She looked down the block toward the mayor's office, hoping to see Josh walking her way. The sidewalk was empty but she turned back in time to see two people enter her store. Customers. "Umm, I need to get inside. And I can't really afford to close early since it's a good day today. I'll be open until eight."

"All right. Then I'll bring dinner to you. Where do you

live?"

She sighed. Maybe tonight would be the better time to talk to Alex, tell him how she felt. "Just come here. I have a table and chairs we can use."

Alex frowned, looking ready to ask her something she didn't want to answer.

"I'm sorry, Alex. I really need to go."

He nodded. "I'll see you tonight."

As Dana called Duffy and headed inside, she couldn't resist another glance up the empty street.

~~~

"Thank you, sir. I'll see you Monday afternoon, then." Josh set his cell phone down and turned in his office chair to stare out the window. He'd set up a meeting with the local tribal council to clarify casino rules and regulations in Washington state. He'd also talked to Sam at the grocery store about his idea. Sam had loved it and immediately started the phone tree. Josh would be meeting with the Willow Bay City Council tomorrow at two to review his hastily-thrown-together feasibility study. Then, at seven, they'd all be at the town meeting to discuss Granson's plan.

And now, Josh had something to offer as an alternative to the resort. It wasn't as big, nor could he promise how effective it would be. But it was a shot, and much more in line with Willow Bay's personality. He could hardly wait to tell Dana.

He slumped further into his chair. The way they'd left things, he wasn't sure she'd want to speak to him, let alone hear any of his ideas. He'd thought of going to see her, to apologize for stepping in where he had no business. He'd chosen to stay away. Having seen clam diggers on the beach during his morning run, he'd hoped business had picked up in town. She'd be busy. At least, that's what he'd told himself.

Friday had flown by, he noticed, glancing at the clock.

Closing up, Josh got in his car and fought the urge to drive by the gift shop. Instead, he drove straight home, not even stopping for his customary end-of-day catch-up with Bernie.

Once inside, he changed into work clothes, grabbed a beer, and went back to hanging sheetrock. By the end of the evening, he had most of the front room rocked in and ready for mud.

Josh sank into his recliner with a fresh beer, wondering what Dana was doing right now. Was she out with Granson? In with Granson? He gripped the soft arms of his chair, wishing he knew. He could drive by Granson's hotel and see if her car was there, though its absence could mean they took his car.

No. Dana would make her own choices and there wasn't a damn thing he could do about it. If she liked flashy...

Once, Josh had aspired to flashy. He'd been a brash twenty-one-year-old who left the small town he'd grown up in for the big city. And not just any big city. Los Angeles. One of the biggest. He'd been so sure he could become an accountant to the stars. He'd thought it all out, made a plan, and presented it to his parents. They hadn't liked him moving so far away, but couldn't argue with his facts. So they gave their blessing and helped him move into a studio apartment above some small but nice office space where he'd started his CPA career.

Getting the right people to notice him, though, hadn't factored into his plan. Four months later, he hadn't landed a single client. A few more months and he'd be heading for home, broke.

Meeting Sandra changed all that. He'd gone to a party to cheer up, but spent the night wallowing in his beer until she appeared, a golden angel with a face as pleasing as the curves of her body.

"Hi, cutie. Anyone sitting here?"

Josh closed his gaping mouth and shook his head. She introduced herself and they spent the next couple of hours chatting. In retrospect, he'd mostly listened. Even her voice was angelic.

When she suggested they go back to his place, he'd been on top of the world. Somewhere, in the recesses of his brain, a thought rose in warning that this wasn't a smart idea. He squashed it and brought Sandra home.

She hadn't robbed him. Well, not that night. And she'd stayed. For a year. As an actress, she'd done some guest spots but was still waiting for her big break. She knew people though, and introduced Josh to them. Before long, he had a solid client list and they'd moved into a nice condo, and him into a bigger office with an assistant.

Sandra had wanted more. Always more. She spent money as quickly as Josh made it. It hadn't been long before the arguments started.

"We need to stick to a budget," he'd said.

"I need to spend money to get noticed," she'd come back with.

Finally, she'd had enough. Josh came home to her suitcases packed and sitting by the door.

"I'm leaving, Josh. We're just not a good fit. And, to be honest, you're holding me back. I need more. I need excitement, not boredom."

He'd tried to get her to stay and talk, but a car horn outside signaled the end to their relationship. He'd watched as she carried her bags out to the dark, sleek car that looked nothing like a taxi, and left.

Her departure turned out to be the best thing for him. He'd sold the practice and the condo and left Los Angeles without a backward glance. He'd driven up the coast, barely seeing anything until he reached Willow Bay. Liking what he saw, he'd stayed. He'd put his money into a small office and a studio rental and let his roots grow.

Josh chuckled. He hadn't let his parents know he'd relocated for six months. They'd supported his move to Los Angeles reluctantly and he'd disappointed them. He had to know he could succeed before he told them he'd thoroughly changed his life.

They'd read him the riot act, then drove up from Hood River and hugged him so tight he'd never doubt their love again.

Family was everything. Josh wanted that for himself. He wanted that for Dana. With Dana. If he couldn't have it, then he'd just have to pour his heart into wishing her well.

Even if it killed him.

~~~

"Wow, you thought of everything." Dana had set up the table and chairs in front of her register in the shop, then disappeared to freshen up. When she'd come back, the table had a cloth over it, a spray of roses lay on the side, candles were lit, and dinner was set out from the restaurant with the best pie. He'd driven forty-five minutes each way to get this food. Her nerves returned full force. How could she knock a guy down who'd done such a nice thing for her?

"Only the best for you," Alex said, pulling out her chair for her. "Though, why we're meeting here, I don't understand. Are you afraid to show me where you live?"

"What makes you think that?"

"Because we're here and not at your home."

Dana chewed on her lip for a minute. Very few people knew she lived in the back of the store, and she planned to keep it that way for as long as the town gossip mill would allow. Still, Alex would be gone in a couple days. What was the harm?

Alex beat her to it. "It's all right. You don't have to tell me if you're uncomfortable about it. Let's just enjoy dinner."

Dana sat down, trying to quash her uneasiness. This was a very romantic dinner. "Alex, this—" She waved her hand over the table.

"Don't say anything. Please, not right now. I want to do this for you. Let's enjoy the evening and see where things might go. No pressure."

Against her better judgment, Dana nodded. And the evening turned into one of conversation. Alex was an interesting man, with a lot of ideas. Some good, some grand, some...well, borderline narcissistic, if she were being truthful. He planned to call the Willow Bay resort Granson's, and it was only the first in a string of planned resorts that would become his empire. The plans still sat under her counter. She really needed to pull them out and look at them.

"And I want you to be part of it, Dana. Please consider it. You and I, running Granson's."

"W-what? You barely know me, and I don't have any experience close to what you need."

"You'll learn. And you'll have me. I want you by my side, Dana. Not just in business, but in life."

Oh, Lord. Was he really asking what she thought he was? Is he nuts? This was way too fast. How could he be thinking this after so short a time? "Alex—"

He covered her hand with his. "I know I said no pressure. Don't say no, at least not without thinking it through. It's sudden, but whenever I feel like I do with you, I act. I've gotten to know you, and we'd be good partners. I want you with me. You could have it all. No more financial worries, everything you ever wanted. It will be yours."

No more financial worries. If Alex knew how in debt she was, he'd probably run for the hills. This was Jett all over again, promising her the moon, saying all the right words. Dana glanced out the window, surprised to see Gladys standing there scowling at her. Before Dana could pull her hand out from beneath Alex's, the old woman shook her head, turned, and pushed her cart out of sight.

Dana sighed. "Alex, I'm flattered. Really. We just met, though. This is too sudden, and I'm settled here. I love my shop and Willow Bay." *And I'd much rather be having this conversation with a certain accountant than with you.*

"I know. Just think about it. We can talk again after the town meeting tomorrow night."

Afraid to give him any encouragement, Dana held back her nod, stood and carried the take-out containers to her garbage. "It's getting late, Alex."

She almost laughed at the chagrined look on his face. "It's just past nine."

"Yes, but we—"

"Roll up the carpets early around here," they said together.

Alex pulled her into his arms. "I'll leave. For tonight. Not willingly, but out of respect."

He kissed her, his lips moving over hers in perfect synchronicity, like he'd taken lessons and was practicing. Perfect movements, but no emotion. Nothing like that kiss with Josh. Not even close.

"I want to stay," Alex said. "I want to be with you in every way, Dana. One of these nights," he said, tucking a lock of hair behind her ear. "Soon."

Then he stepped away and Dana was able to breathe again. After he left, Dana put things away and took Duffy out for his nightly walk. Once the dog had settled back on his bed, Dana went into the darkened store and walked to the front window. Leaning against it, she looked outside at the darkness.

Dana went over the conversation with Alex, realizing he'd never actually asked her for a relationship except for the sex thing. He'd asked her to become a partner. Just what did that entail? Business associates with benefits?

Her life was nothing but a series of conundrums. Stay with Jett or leave? Give up her life to accept Alex's offer, which really wasn't an option as she wasn't emotionally involved? Make the first move with Josh or keep waiting? Josh. It was hard not to compare kisses. Alex's had been perfunctory, Josh's full of emotion and need. In that department, there was no contest. And honestly, if she let her heart rule, she'd race to Josh and lay all her feelings at his feet for him to accept or rip to shreds. Except that hadn't gotten her anywhere with Jett but deeply in debt. Maybe a no-emotion relationship with Alex to resolve all her money woes was the smart way to go. Except that wasn't the kind of person she was. There had to be more to life than business.

She looked around at the aisles of *gingilli*. She'd spent the month after she'd first bought the gift shop revamping it to suit her vision. She'd renamed it Tangerine Treasures after her favorite color. And, if it weren't for the debt Jett had piled on her shoulders, she'd be making ends meet, just barely.

She wasn't ready to give up. On the shop, or on her chances of a life here in Willow Bay. Dana didn't want to leave it, or small-town life, behind. Relief eased her tension, which reassured her. She was making the right choice. She would stick with Willow Bay, her shop, and let the rest of the cards fall where they may. Decision made, Dana went back to her apartment and crawled into bed with one resolution at the front of her mind.

Before tomorrow's meeting, she'd tell Alex no. And she'd talk to Josh.

Chapter Ten

Outside the community center, Dana sat in her car, still in a state of shock. She wasn't sure she could go in. How could she have been so wrong? This morning, over coffee, she'd remembered and finally unrolled Alex's plans, promptly spilling her coffee all over them.

Granson's wasn't a resort. It was a small city. Complete with gift shops. No one would ever have to leave. Who needed the beach or the town when you had climate-controlled fun of every sort at your fingertips? His plan wouldn't lift Willow Bay. It would bury it deep beneath the sand like a tsunami.

Josh had been right about everything. And Dana had been an idiot, blinded by debt and her own stupid concerns. She needed to tell Alex what she thought of his plans, and she really needed to tell Josh.

When her phone rang, she jumped. "Hi, Aimi."

"Hey, I know your big meeting is tonight and I just wanted to wish you luck. I know you've been pinning your hopes on this new resort."

"Oh, Aimi. I've been so stupid," Dana cried.

"What's wrong?"

"Josh was right. The resort will wipe out Willow Bay.

It's too big, too self-contained."

"So go in there and say so."

"How can I? I've been touting this as the best option for us. I've let Alex use me like a puppet. Oh, God. He even asked me to 'partner' with him on this venture. And in life."

"Oh, my God. Did he mean it?"

The tears wouldn't stop as Dana shrugged. "How do I know? Everything I thought was good...isn't." *And who you thought was wrong, wasn't.* She hung her head.

"Well, then, tell them what you think."

"How can I?"

"Simple. Say 'I made a mistake.'"

Dana took big gulping breaths, trying to calm herself. The tap on her window startled her and she screamed. Josh stood there, concern written in the deep furrowed lines on his face.

"What's happened?" Aimi asked.

"Josh is here."

"Go, talk to him. We'll finish this later."

Dana put her phone in her purse and opened her car door with shaking hands.

Josh immediately pulled her into his arms. "What's wrong, sweetheart?"

The tears threatened again and Dana hung on tight, trying to calm down enough to tell him. They just stood there like that, rocking back and forth, while she tried to find her voice.

"Shit," he mumbled.

"What?" Dana raised her head to look up at him.

"Granson's coming."

"Shit."

Josh tightened his hold on her, but Dana pushed back so she could see him. "Before he gets here. You were right about everything, Josh. I'm so sorry."

"About—"

"There's my girl," Alex said as Dana stepped back.

Dana cringed when Alex put his arm around her waist. Josh took a step forward, fists clenched. She gave Josh a quick shake of her head. *My fight.* Then she looked at Alex. "Get your arm from around my waist, please."

"Whoa. What's this all about? Having second thoughts?" He smiled. Gloated, more like.

Nope. No second thoughts here. Once Dana made the decision, everything fell into place for her. How could she have ever even considered him as someone she wanted in her life?

Out of the corner of her eye, Dana could see Josh's fisted hands. She needed to talk to him, explain. But first, she had to set Alex straight.

"I've invited Dana to join me in this venture. And more," Alex told Josh, reaching for Dana, who side-stepped him.

Dana closed her eyes for a moment. If she tried to set Alex straight now, he and Josh might end up in a fistfight.

"I don't plan—" Dana tried to explain.

"We can have a long talk right after the meeting," Alex said.

Dana fumed. The man kept cutting her off and she'd had it. "Alex, we're talking now."

"No time, darling." Alex turned toward Josh. "Ready to put my resort to a vote?"

"I think you should stop being rude to Dana and hear her out."

"I will, I will. We'll have a long talk after we get done with this town meeting."

Dana settled a hand on Josh's arm. "It's okay. I can wait until then."

The look on Josh's face said he didn't think he could.

Thankfully, he didn't pursue it. "I'm more than ready to take you on," he said to Alex, smiling.

Dana could see the smile didn't reach his eyes.

"You sound pretty sure of yourself."

"I'm sure of this town."

"Well, I know you're not too thrilled with my idea. I'd wish you luck, but... Come on, Dana. Let's get settled inside."

He nudged her toward the building. Dana pulled away and walked beside him, glancing over her shoulder at Josh, trying to show with a look everything she felt, how wrong she'd been. He stood there, stiff as a board, anger tightening his face. Alex first. She'd set him straight, then lay it all out with Josh and take her lumps. She didn't want to lose Josh but it was time for some honesty from her. He'd more than earned that.

"I can hardly wait for this meeting to be over with," Alex said. "I'm anxious to start construction."

"You've got more hoops to go through before that can happen. Environmental studies, traffic studies. Stuff like that."

"All done. We break ground week after next."

Dana stopped in her tracks. "How can that happen so fast?"

Alex shrugged. "Because I'm good at what I do and I know who to talk to."

"No, this can't be. You couldn't have done this so quickly."

"Things move fast in my world. You'll have to get used to that." Alex started walking again, but Dana stayed put until he stopped and walked back to her.

"You never told me how big your plans were, Alex. Willow Bay will become a ghost town on the edge of your resort if you go through with this."

"This whole area will thrive because of me. I'm bringing

life back to Willow Bay."

"No, you're not. You misled me into believing this wasn't the all-inclusive resort you have planned. I've looked at the specs. There will be no reason for people to ever leave the land you build on. I want no part of it. Or you."

"Well," he said after a pause, showing no emotion whatsoever, "that's your choice. But you're missing out on a big opportunity."

"I won't support you in there."

"Then you'll be a laughing stock, because you've already supported me all over town. Now, I'm going inside to prepare. I'll save you a seat. It's up to you if you want to use it or not."

Dana watched him walk off. How could she have ever gotten on board with a plan like this? Alex was... Dana felt the blood drain from her face. Definitely like Jett. Flashy, all about the glitz, all about the money. Oh, God. Dana followed him at a slow pace, berating herself the whole way, wondering if Josh would ever forgive her for supporting Alex's plan. She looked back. Josh was talking to Sam, so any discussion between them would have to wait until later.

Choosing a chair near the front, but not up on the stage, Dana saw Alex frown when she didn't join him. Tough.

Josh walked in with Sam and stopped short when Dana caught his eye. There was no time to give him a head's up as he joined Alex on stage.

Dana didn't know what to do. Alex was right. She'd vouched for him and his plan to the people of Willow Bay. She had to come clean, tell the community she'd come to love that she'd made a mistake. Would they accept her apology or consider her a gold-digger? It didn't matter. She had to come out against Alex's plan and give Josh her full support. She'd look like a fool, but it was the right thing to do.

It was going to be a very long night.

~~~

Anger and embarrassment were written all over Dana's face, so plain Josh could see her distress from his seat on the stage. He wanted to console her, to make whatever pain she was feeling go away. What had happened over the last few days that filled her with so much turmoil? Emotion deepened the furrows of her forehead and he wanted to erase those lines. Damn. If she'd only let him in.

You were right about everything.

What did that mean? Granson had shown up at the worst possible time. When he interrupted Dana yet again, the malice-filled smile he'd given Josh made Josh want to punch the arrogant ass. It took every ounce of strength to stop himself from yanking Dana to his side. She was a strong woman who could make her own choices. He needed to remember that, but protecting her meant everything to him. Josh wanted her in his arms, to comfort, to love, to be together forever. They were right for each other. He knew it. Now he needed Dana to understand it, too.

The community center had filled up with just about everyone from town, by Josh's recollection. This decision was important and they all knew it.

Except it wasn't so important anymore. Not to Josh. He didn't want to be at this meeting at all. He wanted to be with Dana. One thing was certain, though. After this was over, he and Dana were going to have a serious heart-to-heart. It was time to lay it all on the line.

He tapped a gavel on the table, bringing the volume down several notches.

"Hello. It's good to see so many people here." Josh glanced around the room at the expectant faces and couldn't help but frown at Dana's continued worried look. Granson, on the other hand, looked smug and assured of the outcome.

"As you know," Josh continued, "Alexander Granson"—Josh gestured to him—" has come to Willow Bay with a plan to build a resort. This meeting is to put forward the pros and cons of the endeavor."

"There are no cons," Granson interjected with a smile.

"That may be so, but we should, as a town, see the plans and make a joint decision about its viability."

"If it'll give my business a kick start, I'm all for it," someone hollered from the back.

"Jim, is that you?" Josh asked. He owned the bait and tackle shop and made sure to voice his opinion, usually negative, about every change the town considered.

"You bet it is."

"Okay, well, we'll have a vote at the end of the meeting, but right now, I'd like to show you the plan."

Granson leaned into the microphone. "Actually, I've brought a presentation with me."

"Well, get on with it," Jim said.

"I'd love to."

He had a presentation? Josh glanced at Dana, who looked as surprised as he did. The screen was already in place because Josh, unbeknownst to Granson, had his own presentation. Granson waved to someone on the side, presumably the person with the laptop, and the lights dimmed. He clicked the remote in his hand and the screen came to life as words scrolled by.

Granson's.

A place for singles.

A place for couples.

A place for families.

Come play at the ocean.

Josh craned his neck as the picture took shape. It was Granson's plan, but at the same time, it wasn't. It was like everything had been made to appear smaller. He could see the edges of the cannery property and nothing but walking paths over most of the area. The hotel looked smaller as well and there was no indication of a casino.

Five minutes later, even Josh was almost convinced the project would rescue Willow Bay. Granson was good at what he did.

"So you see," Granson said as the lights came up, "there's just enough here to bring people to this town. A lot of people. Visitors equal thriving businesses, and that makes Willow Bay's future very bright."

Murmurs of assent rolled through the audience. Dana had taken to wringing her hands.

Josh stood up, smiling at his opponent when he didn't want to. "That's a great presentation, Mr. Granson. I've brought one of my own, though it's not as polished as yours."

Josh motioned to Sam who switched out computers and loaded Josh's PowerPoint presentation, then lowered the lights again. The first slide was the overall plan for resort.

Granson stiffened as the slide came up. "That's privileged information, mayor. You can't share that with the general public."

"Why can't this be shared?" Josh said into the mic. "It's their town. You want them to have all the facts, don't you?"

After a perusal of the expectant sea of faces in the audience, Granson sank back into his chair with a scowl.

Josh, mic in hand, walked across the stage. Using a laser pointer, he began to outline the cannery property on the screen. "As you can see here, the plans call for the resort to be built out to the very edge of the property." He looked at the people, his friends, and used Granson's own words against him. "That makes this place bigger than the theme parks in California."

Mumblings resonated through the hall.

"The hotel, according to these plans, is fifteen stories tall. There are indoor and outdoor water parks. And, if you follow these walking paths, you'll see gift shops, urgent care, even a grocery store."

Sam grunted.

"These are long-range plans," Granson said, standing. "The first stage will only be a five-story hotel and water park."

"What's the timeline for these long-range plans?" Sam asked.

"Five years," Granson said, his voice muted.

"So in five years, Willow Bay becomes redundant?" Connie asked. "Why would people visit my café when there are"—she pointed, counting—" at least four restaurants inside your complex."

"Resort," Granson said. "And competition is good for business."

"Not when people don't ever have to leave your property."

"And that's not all," Josh said, deciding to drop his bombshell. "I noticed there were a couple pages left out of the plans."

Granson reddened.

"Yes," Josh said. "They are numbered. I reached out to the architect and told him who I was and that Alex Granson had given me the plans to review. He was more than happy to provide me with the missing pages."

Anger didn't sit well with Alex Granson, who squirmed in his chair as Josh hit the button for the next slide. The plans for a not-so-small casino popped up on the screen.

A collective gasp ran through the audience.

"How can you have a such a large casino, Mr. Granson?" asked Connie "I thought the law allowed something of this magnitude on native lands only."

"Everything here is legal." Granson's smile was tight. "Everything. You won't be able to beat this in court because I didn't break a single law." He stood. "Sure, there's a casino. There has to be adult fun and family fun. That's the way to bring tourists in."

Josh glanced at the mostly frowning audience. They weren't happy. Good. Josh needed them aware of all the ramifications.

Granson straightened. "Do whatever you want, vote however you need to, but this is going to happen." He walked straight to Josh. Putting his hand over the mic, he forced it down. "It's a done deal, mayor. I was trying to be nice, but the property is mine, the plans have been approved, and the heavy equipment moves in next week." His eyes gleamed. "There's nothing you can do to stop this. Nothing at all."

"Then why the farce of trying to get the town's approval?"

"It's always easier when the locals are on your side. But this will be done whether these people are happy or not. And you, as mayor, can't do a damn thing to stop it."

Granson let go of the mic and stomped out of the community center.

Josh moved slowly back to the center of the stage. If what Granson said was true, everything Josh had done was for naught. He slumped down onto a chair. He stayed there for a long moment, until he felt a hand on his shoulder. When he looked up, it was into Dana's soulful, dark brown eyes.

"What did he say to you, Josh?"

Josh sat up. "That it's a done deal. Construction starts next week."

Dana blanched. "He can't. Not this fast."

"We've been hoodwinked. He was buying time for the

rest of the permits. I'm certain of it now." Josh shook his head. "He must have greased a lot of palms to get this through so fast, and skirted legalities."

Dana sat down next to Josh.

"Hey, Dana," someone called out. "Weren't you helping that guy Granson peddle his resort idea?"

Josh heard her intake of breath.

Yeah," someone else said. "You believe in this thing, don't you? You told us all it was a good idea."

After two deep breaths, Dana looked out over the audience and picked up the mic. "I did. And I'm so very sorry." She looked at Josh. "I had no idea until this morning. I never looked at the plans until then. That was stupid of me. I'm so, so sorry."

"We came to this meeting hoping for a better future and this isn't it," Jim said, coming forward from the back. "We're let down now, and that's your fault, Dana Ricci. You led us to believe this would be good for the town when you never even looked at the plans."

"Dana's hurting just as much as the rest of us," Connie said. "Give her the same benefit you'd give any of us locals."

Blushes could be pretty or ugly. Dana's wasn't pretty. Red splotches covered her face and neck as she stared at Jim. Tears slipped from the corners of her eyes.

Josh got up to help her, but she stayed him with her hand. "You're right. I screwed up. I'm apologizing to you, Jim, and to all of Willow Bay. You're my family and I—I let you down. I can't tell you how sorry I am."

"That doesn't do us any good," Jim said." Not only are we not better off, we'll be worse off if this hoity-toity plan goes through."

"Hey," Josh said, fully intending to defend Dana.

"No, Josh. He's right," Dana said. "We'd have seen through this ruse much faster if I hadn't gotten lost in the financial end of things."

Josh reached for her hand, but she yanked it away and ran straight out of the building.

He wanted to follow her. He needed to reassure her, but he wasn't done with the meeting. He had a town to calm down. A town that was getting louder and louder by the second.

He picked up the mic. "If everyone could have a seat, I have more to explain."

A lot of grumbling ensued, but almost everyone sat down. Jim stood against the wall beside the door, arms folded over his chest, ready to bolt if he didn't like what he heard.

"I have a proposition."

That got their attention.

Chapter Eleven

It took Josh very little time after Saturday's meeting to tell himself boring be damned. If Dana thought he was boring, she'd have to tell him to his face. The town had gotten on board his Beer and Chowder Festival bandwagon with enthusiasm. The idea was good and he'd pulled it together quickly. Boring was a subjective term and Josh rejected that word as applying to him. He prayed Dana would, too. His life was anything but ordinary and he wanted her in it.

By Monday morning, though, he was beside himself with worry. He'd called Dana enough times to be considered a full-fledged stalker, had left a bunch of messages. She hadn't picked up, hadn't called him back. And her store remained dark, even though it was after eleven. She hadn't opened yesterday, either, which was more than strange considering there were clam diggers in town.

Where the hell was she?

He'd driven by the store twice already this morning, so this time, he parked and went into the café.

"Hey, mayor," Connie said from behind the counter.

There were a few customers, all locals Josh knew, and each waved or said hi. Connie brought him his coffee and settled into the booth opposite him.

"That was some meeting Saturday," she said.

"I wish it had gone better."

Old Ben spoke from the next booth. "Went as well as it could, son. I couldn't have run it any better."

"Is this resort really a done deal?" Connie worried the rag tucked into her apron.

"Yeah, my question exactly," Jim said, coming to stand beside them, along with the others in the café.

Josh looked at each one of them. Friends, all, even if Jim did like to argue for the sake of arguing. Josh genuinely liked everyone in Willow Bay. They were family and the weight of taking care of them lay heavy on his shoulders.

"The only information I have about impending ground-breaking is from Granson himself," Josh said. He didn't trust the man, but tried to stick to the facts. Willow Bay didn't need the protests. They had enough problems at the moment. Josh glanced across the street. Still dark.

"I've got some calls in, and a meeting with the tribal council. Granson seems to think this is a done deal. I'm not so sure, but I need more time to...learn things."

"That resort will bury us," Jim said.

"Night before last, you were all for it," Connie said, slapping him lightly with the rag.

"That's because he made it look perfect. And that new gal"—Jim cocked his head in the direction of Dana's shop—" helped him."

"New gal? She's been here for six months, Jim," Josh said. "She's as much one of us as I am."

"You been here a lot longer than her. And you're smart. You think things through and ask our opinions."

"Dana is smart," Josh said, hackles raising. Smart and beautiful and funny and full of life.

"She took Granson's side before she knew what he was

really planning," Connie said, giving Jim a stare. "We can't fault Dana for wanting to help this town make some money."

"Help herself, more likely," Jim said.

"If all you're going to do is play the blame game, then you can just get out of my café. We don't speak ill of people in here, especially those who are hurting as much as we are."

Damn it. Jim would be happy to spread his cantankerous discontent around town. Josh didn't want Dana to have to deal with it. He needed to nip this in the bud. "Look, I think Dana was swept along because she's got some financial troubles."

"We're all hurting," Jim said.

Josh didn't want to say too much. Hell, he didn't *know* very much. Dana wouldn't let him in long enough to help. "Whatever's going on with her, it's bad, and it's making her do things she normally wouldn't do, but she's a good person. Deep down, you know that. She cares about this town."

Jim snorted. "She doesn't understand what it takes to live here." He handed Connie some money. "I've gotta get back to work. Thanks for the food, Connie. Good as always."

He left without a backward glance.

Josh turned to Connie and the rest of the folks who'd gathered around. "Jim is wrong. Dana's good people. The kind of people this town needs. Give her a chance."

Everyone went back to their tables. Thankfully, with less grumbling than Josh expected.

"I know you're sweet on Dana," Connie said.

"That's not—"

Connie raised her hand. "Hear me out. You need to make sure you don't have those rose-colored glasses on. That you see the real Dana."

"She apologized, Connie. Right there at the meeting, to everyone. She felt horrible. I could see the agony in her face.

Couldn't you?"

"Yes. And that's why she gets the benefit of the doubt from me. But I need to know you're thinking with the part of you this town relies on. Your brain."

"I'm doing what I think is best for Willow Bay."

She patted his hand and stood up. "I like you, Josh. You're one of the reasons Willow Bay's heart is so strong. I know you'll do what's right."

"Thanks, Connie." Josh needed all the encouragement he could get. He glanced across the street at Tangerine Treasures. Still dark. Damn it.

He stood. His meeting with the tribal council was in a couple hours and he needed to get to the office and pull some things together.

"Josh," Connie said as he paid his bill. "Thanks for plugging my chowder at the meeting. Your Beer and Chowder festival is a great idea."

He chuckled. "Funny thing there. Wasn't my idea."

"Whose was it?"

"Gladys's"

"Well, I'll be. I always give her a cup of chowder when she stops in to help her warm-up."

"She loves it," Josh said.

"I wish we could get her beneath a roof."

"Me, too, Connie. Me, too. Have a nice rest of your day." Josh waved to the two other patrons and left the café thinking about Gladys and Dana and Granson's town-killing resort. He had loads to worry about and very few helpful answers.

When he pulled into the parking lot at his office, he was surprised to see a blue car sitting there.

Dana's car.

~~~

Hell looked better than Dana did at the moment. She

looked in the rearview mirror. Her face was blotchy, her eyes swollen. She'd spent the best part of the last couple days wallowing in self-pity. It was time to pick herself up. She'd driven there intending to lay it all out for Josh. But now that he'd pulled in, her nerves wavered. She should leave. But no. He had a right to understand why she'd done what she'd done. She opened the car door.

Duffy leaped out and barreled around the back of the car to jump into Josh's open arms.

"Duffy!" Dana yelled. The rain had returned in earnest and Josh's suit jacket was soon a muddy mess. "Get down!"

"It's okay, Dana. Come on. Let's get in out of this rain."

Josh unlocked his door and pushed it open, still holding Duffy. Dana shut the door as she followed him in, afraid to move and drip all over his floor. She'd left her place so quickly, she hadn't grabbed a coat or even sensible shoes. She looked down at her flip-flops.

Josh grabbed a rag from the bin he kept near the door and vigorously rubbed Duffy. "You look a bit drowned yourself," he told Dana, tossing her a towel-sized rag.

She believed him. Drying off as best she could, she slipped out of her flip-flops.

"Go on in the office. I'll make us some coffee to warm up."

"That sounds good." Really good, she thought as she shivered. In Josh's office, she sank into one corner of the small couch, pulling her feet up underneath her. She pulled the throw blanket around her shoulders. It smelled like Josh, which made her smile. Did he sleep here some nights?

"Here you go." He handed her a steaming mug and she cupped the warmth.

"Thanks."

He sat down beside her on the couch. "I've been calling you ever since the meeting."

"I know. I—I had some things to figure out before I could talk to anyone, let alone you."

He stiffened. "Let alone me?"

"I didn't mean it that way." Dana shook her head. This wasn't beginning well. "I need to come clean, Josh. With you, more than anybody else. You're important to me, and I care what you think."

"I—"

"No. Let me talk first, please. I need to get this out while I have the courage."

He opened his mouth, then closed it, raising his mug in her direction, giving her the chance she'd asked for. Dana smelled her coffee, buying time, collecting her thoughts.

"I'm not sure where to start."

"How about at the beginning?" he said quietly.

That was as good a place as any. "I was married before. Did you know that?"

By the surprise on his face, that would be a negative.

"I was. For two years. Jett, my ex... Well, we both grew up in Spokane, went to the same high school. He was one of the popular people. Me, not so much. So, when we ran into each other one night a couple years after high school and he paid attention to me, I was flattered. Not just flattered. I fell. Hard. I knew Spokane was too small for him. He was larger than life, but I thought I could tame him, bring him enough happiness that he'd choose to stay. I tried. I worked hard at my jobs."

"Jobs?"

"Yes. I had three of them. Jett never could find the right fit for his...brilliance, so I was the primary earner." She sipped her coffee to wet her dry mouth. "He, as it turned out, was the primary spender. After two years, I'd had enough. We had a big fight and he said he was leaving for the big city and I could come or stay, whatever I wanted."

Josh's lips were thin lines.

"I stayed. I never heard from him again until last week. Technically, I still haven't heard from him, and it's been over two years."

"What did you hear last week?"

"I got a letter from some attorney in New York." Dana gulped her coffee. This was the hard part. This was where Josh would either stay or run. Her hands started to shake.

Josh took the mug from her and set it on the end table. He tipped her chin up with one finger while reaching for her hand with the other. "Nothing you tell me could possibly change how I feel about you."

"Don't be so sure," she whispered.

"Then get it out. Let's deal with it." Josh took a deep breath. He held her hands between his own, gently, supportively.

"Jett apparently moved to New York City. He amassed $200,000 in debt."

"What does that have to do with you?"

"He did it in my name."

"But you're divorced, right?"

"I never filed, so no, we're not divorced."

Dana closed her eyes, waiting for his hands to tighten on hers. Or worse, let them go. Neither happened. After several long seconds, she opened her eyes and looked at Josh. He looked serious, but not scared. Not ready to flee or utter those final words—I can't deal with this. He looked accepting. How?

"Have you filed for divorce now?" he asked quietly.

"Y-Yes. Last week."

"And do you have someone helping you with the attorney thing? Because he can't make you responsible for that debt."

Dana nodded. "My friend Aimi in Spokane. She's an

attorney. Family law, but she's helping me on this."

"Good." He shook her hands gently to emphasize the word.

"No, it's not." Dana shook her head. "The attorney in New York will make good on this threat. Josh, they can take the store."

He pulled her into his arms. "They can't."

"Aimi says they aren't budging."

"Honey, you do understand that this is my wheelhouse, right?"

"I couldn't tell you, Josh. I didn't want you to find out what a screwup my life is. I respect you too much."

"Look at me, Dana."

She did, staring into blue eyes that held so much emotion.

"I *respect* you, too, Dana Ricci. And this isn't your screwup. Well, maybe the divorce thing is."

"I was waiting until I had an address so I could let him know. If I was going to end our marriage, he had a right to know."

"That's the Dana I know and love. The one who always thinks of others before herself."

Love? Did he just say love?

Josh kissed her then. What started as a slow, healing kiss deepened into a reckoning of months lost to misconceptions and pride. Dana settled into his embrace, pouring all her emotions into the kiss, into her hand on his chest, telling him she loved him back with actions instead of words.

When Josh finally broke the kiss, they were both breathing heavily. "You are the best kisser, Dana Ricci."

"Good inspiration," she said, smiling.

"Now, uh," he shook his head, "back to what's going on in your life. You do understand that finances are what I do, right?"

"Yes, Josh. I—I didn't want you to know how bad I'd let things get."

"Would you be willing to let me go over your books, see what I can do?"

Dana gulped. The time had come to take the plunge or run for the hills. If she'd learned anything from Jett and Granson, it was that she was done running. "Yes. I'd appreciate any help you're willing to give, as long as we do it together."

"Thank you. I know that wasn't easy." Josh pulled her in close again, glancing at his watch. "Damn. I'm close to being late for a meeting with the tribal council."

"Go," Dana said. "We can finish this later."

He kissed her, soft and slow. "You can just bet we'll finish this later."

"Good luck, Josh. I hope they help you stop Granson."

"Me, too." Josh grabbed a file from his desk and headed for the door, turning before he left. "Want to come along?"

Dana's heart filled to overflowing to hear him ask her to help bring Granson down. She had a score to settle. "You bet!"

Chapter Twelve

The drive home from the meeting with the local tribe was quiet. Josh had a lot to think over. He imagined Dana did as well. No one, including the native tribes, had been aware of a gambling license issued to Granson Industries for use in Washington state. They'd done some digging since current laws did not allow for Granson's plans. Somehow, he'd circumvented those prohibitions and his permit appeared to be legal. "Appeared" being the operative word. The council had vowed to find out how this had happened without their knowledge.

As Josh drove back to town, he tried to figure out how they could delay the start of construction until this could be sorted out. Staring out the window at the rain, he saw the sign before he could read it. When he read the first words, he slammed on the brakes, putting his hand out to stop Dana from slamming forward.

"Ooomph!" Dana said. "Why did we stop?"

"Look," Josh said, pointing as he put the car in park.

"Oh, my God," Dana whispered.

A billboard-sized sign at the edge of the cannery property showcased the grand resort. "Granson's," it said, in harsh, blinking neon. "While away the hours in luxury.

Coming soon."

"That had to have been put up in the three or so hours we've been gone," Josh said.

Dana hid her face in her hands. "I wish I'd seen through his façade right from the beginning. I feel like I helped make this mess."

Josh peeled her hands away. "This isn't your fault."

"But the whole town must hate me for telling them this was a good thing."

Josh thought of Jim and his aggravation. "There might be a few fences to mend. But the people here know you have a big heart and you were only trying to help. This will blow over."

"Or pile-drive me the rest of the way into the ground."

He turned her to look at him. "You've been here long enough to know this town. They won't desert you."

"They should. I'm a complete mess."

"Not from where I'm sitting." He kissed her, a brief reminder of the door they'd opened. One that he wanted to close, with them on the same side—in her bedroom. "How about we go back to your place?"

Dana chewed her lip and Josh frowned. He thought they'd hashed everything out. Was there something else?

"Head for the store."

"I'd rather head for a bed. Even a comfortable couch will do."

"Just head for the store, Josh. Trust me, you'll understand soon. Besides, I need to let Duffy out."

Once at the store, she led Josh through the dark interior. He could hear Duffy scratching at the rear door. When she opened it, the dog leaped out and ran circles around them both.

Josh laughed as Dana went down on a knee to try to tame him as light poured in from the open door. When Josh stepped through to give Dana some room, he stopped in shock.

"This is where you live?"

Dana shrugged, holding Duffy. "It's comfortable and saves on expenses."

He walked around, taking in the microwave, burner, mini-fridge. All this time, he'd never known. No wonder she'd answered every time he called the store.

"Your cell is the store phone, isn't it?"

"Again, saves money."

"I can appreciate that," he said, looking at what appeared to be a very comfortable queen bed, then back at Dana. Joining her, he set Duffy on the ground and pulled Dana into his arms, where he'd wanted her to be forever.

God, she felt good. So damn good, even with Duffy jumping on them. Her eyes darkened as she looked up into his. "I, umm, need to take Duffy out."

"Yes," he said, backing up reluctantly. "Let's do it together."

After slipping her dog into his harness, they used the back door and headed for the beach.

"It's stopped raining," Dana said.

"Not for long."

Dana laughed.

Josh reached for her hand, pulling it into his pocket for warmth. Once they saw no other hardy souls walking the beach, Dana let Duffy run free. Josh turned her toward him, pulling both her hands between them to warm them up. Some hair had slipped out from her knit cap and he reached up to tuck it in and pull the cap lower over her ears. He stroked her cheek.

"You are a beautiful woman, Dana Ricci."

She laid her head on his chest.

"You are. Believe me, with those soft, inviting chocolate

eyes, and that rich, dark hair." God, he'd wanted to run his hands through that waste-length hair for so long. "It's impossible to be sad around your smile, and your heart is so big you're always looking to help others before yourself. There's so much good in you."

"Why didn't you tell me any of this before?"

"I never felt good enough for you. You are full of energy and sass and goodness. I'm..." Boring. He couldn't say the word, but it was there on the tip of his tongue.

"You're what?"

He sighed. "That's a story for another time. Right now, I really want to do this."

"What?"

He touched his lips to hers. Felt her body sigh as she leaned in. Deepened the kiss. This felt so right. She felt so right. Soft, molded to him, she opened her lips and he accepted the invitation, tasting, putting all his feelings into this discovery.

When he pulled away, Dana leaned further in as if unwilling to break the contact. She shook her head and looked around, then chuckled.

"What?" Josh asked.

"This is where you kissed me the first time."

She was right. This was just about the exact same place.

"Then this just became our spot, though we might not want to put up a sign or bench."

"No. That might lead to others trying to claim it."

"And it's all ours."

Duffy chose that moment to jump up on their legs, wet sand and all. Laughing, Dana put his leash on and they went back to her shop. Together, they toweled Duffy off and fed him.

"We should get some dinner," Josh said. "Want to go to the café?"

Dana cocked her head. "I'm not sure I'm ready to see what the town thinks of me just yet. Besides, I don't think I want to share you."

Josh's eyes widened and the thrill of his need to be with her pulsed through him. He pulled Dana into his arms again. "I want that, too. How about I run across the street to get us some food and we eat here?"

"That sounds perfect. I'll set the table."

Josh looked around. "What table?"

"Well, you'll just have to wait and see, won't you. Now shoo, because ever since you mentioned dinner, my stomach's been growling."

"All right," he said, laughing. "Do you want your usual?"

"You know what my usual is?"

"Dinner salad without tomatoes, chicken on top, blue cheese dressing on the side."

Dana put her hands on her hips. "Have you been stalking me, Josh Morgan?"

"Did you happen to notice all the calls from me on your phone for the last two days? Of course, I've been stalking you."

He headed out into the shop just as a pillow went flying by him. Though the rain had started again, he nearly skipped through the puddles on his jog to the café. Even Granson's neon blinking sign two blocks away couldn't dampen his spirits.

This might not be an actual date, but Josh was going to take it as such. This was the beginning he'd waited for and he had no plans to squander it.

~~~

Dana pulled the antique table away from the wall and bent up the wings to form a round dining table. It fit in her room, just barely, and if things went any further than that kiss after dinner, they probably ought to put the table away first. Still, there was a specialness to tonight that she wanted to honor. So she got out her one tablecloth, red-checkered. She set out candles, plates, and opened the one bottle of wine she had, a gift from Aimi when she'd moved here.

In her bathroom, she freshened up and changed from jeans into black leggings. She spritzed perfume along her neck. *Does Josh have any allergies?* Panicked because she didn't know, she grabbed a washcloth and scrubbed as much of the scent off as she could, then pulled on a turquoise turtleneck tunic, the one that fit her the best. Brushing her hair, she left it down instead of in her perennial ponytail. She ran her fingers through the strands, wishing they were Josh's fingers, hoping they would be.

When the bell tinkled, Dana went out to lock the front door behind Josh. Back in her room, he set the food down on the side table and looked around. "Wow, you work fast."

"I wanted tonight to be special."

Josh ran his hands along Dana's arms, causing her to shiver with delight. "It already is." He kissed her, a miserly short kiss. "If we do any more kissing," he said," we won't eat dinner."

Dana sighed. He was right. Her stomach grumbled its opinion and they both laughed.

"Why don't you pour the wine. You like red, right?"

"Red is my preference."

"Great. I'll set the food out." She opened the Styrofoam containers and smiled. BLT and fries. "I'm not the only creature of habit," she said as she transferred Josh's dinner to a plate and handed it to him, got hers, and sat down.

"A BLT has everything. Protein, carbs, vegetables. It's the perfect meal."

"If you like bacon."

The look of shock on Josh's face was priceless. "You

don't like bacon?"

"I do. My hips don't."

His eyes lit up. "Your hips look just fine to me."

"Because I rarely indulge in bacon, thank you very much."

"That's criminal."

"It isn't. Really." Dana leaned forward. "Because when I do eat bacon, I savor it. Life is too short and I don't want to deny myself. I just need to be mindful about some things."

With a gleam in his eye, Josh leaned in, running a finger along her cheek. "And do you have to be mindful about me?"

"I fully intend to glut my senses with you," she whispered, turning into his hand.

The intensity in Josh's blue eyes drew Dana in. She wanted to stay here forever, to just be with Josh and not care about anything else. Just the two of them. Together.

"Do you trust me?" Josh asked, his eyes dipping to her lips.

She didn't hesitate. "Yes."

"Close your eyes."

She did, without reservation. His fingers caressed her lips in such a way that Dana felt the tingle throughout her body. He nudged her mouth open and set something on her tongue.

What?

Dana closed her mouth and tasted—bacon. Her eyes flew open and Josh, still leaning forward, smiled widely. "Indulge."

"Oh, you!" she said, sitting back, trying to recover some equilibrium as her very needy body righted itself. The taste of bacon got through to her and she chewed slowly, savoring the taste. "Okay, okay, it's good."

He sat back, laughing. "I don't know where Connie gets

her bacon, but I've never had better."

"I can see why you're hooked on her BLTs." Still, there were things she wanted more than bacon. Her body thrummed with a desire to be closer to Josh. To explore him, to be explored.

He stood up suddenly.

"What is it?" Dana asked.

"Let's clear the dishes."

"Why the big hurry?" She stood and handed her plate to him, holding on to it while waiting for his answer.

"Because dinner's over and I want dessert."

The intensity of his gaze proved to Dana what dessert he had in mind. She smiled. "Me, too."

They quickly cleared the table and she was in Josh's arms, right where she wanted to be. He kissed her forehead, peppered kisses alongside her eye, down her cheek, along her chin, until finally, he claimed her mouth. What started as a gentle reckoning quickly grew to a fierce need to explore, and the mild-mannered Josh she thought she knew took charge, claiming her with his lips and tongue. Inciting threads of fire that radiated through her body to settle in that one place she so desperately wanted him to touch. Dana clung to him, her hands moving down his back, over his hips, then back up to run through his hair.

When his hand grazed the side of her breast, Dana realized he wasn't still, either. He cupped her and she arched into him with need. He took advantage and kissed her neck in that oh-so-sweet spot. Josh tried to move downward, but her turtleneck stopped him, so Dana stepped back and slowly pulled the tunic over her head. She stood there in her bra, clutching the shirt, knowing her breasts were too small, chewing her lower lip as she went down the list of everything that was wrong with her body.

That list didn't show in Josh's eyes. Instead, they were

glazed with the sheen of tears. Tears? What had she done to make him cry?

"You are so beautiful, Dana Ricci. So flawless that I'm almost afraid to touch you."

With those words, Dana shoved her subconscious into a box. Leave it to Josh to say exactly what she needed to hear. Dana smiled and walked back into his arms. She stared up at him.

"If you don't touch me everywhere soon, Joshua Morgan, I'm going to explode."

After a brief hint of surprise, Josh's lopsided smile returned, along with the intensity in those bright blue eyes. "Oh, I'm going to touch you all over, all right," he said, his voice low and beckoning. "I've waited a long time to get to know every curve of your body and I fully intend to explore."

They looked into each other's eyes, their smiles fading as desire took the lead. Like a slow-motion video, Josh lowered his lips to touch hers. Gentle ended there, as he possessed her with his mouth, and she gladly let him in. Somehow, they made it to the bed and he trailed kisses from her neck along her bra strap to the top of her demi-bra.

"I like the lace," he said.

"I thought you might."

He reached behind her, undid her bra, and smoothed it away from her body. "But not as much as you, bare."

Josh sat up, yanked his shirt off, and held himself above her for a long moment.

"So beautiful." He lowered his mouth to her breast and Dana forgot all about thought, so many sensations poured through her. Spikes of need ravaged her core as he kissed, sucked, licked with his talented tongue. Dana pressed his head to her, needing more, needing everything.

When she thought she couldn't take one more moment, he moved to her other breast and she arched into him, overcome by sensations she'd never known before.

The muscles in his back moved as she ran her hands over them, learning, getting to know him. But she needed more. So much more.

"Josh—"

He raised his head.

"I need—"

His palm cupped her core, adding pressure. She about came off the bed.

"Oh, God, yes. I need you. In me. Now."

He chuckled. "We've got a ways to go before that point."

"I don't need foreplay. Please. I just need you."

"Oh, honey," he said, his eyes darkening. "We haven't even started foreplay. These are just the opening moves. Hips up."

He slowly peeled down her leggings, then pulled off his jeans. For the first time in all the months she'd known him, Dana knew just how fine a body Josh had. Lean, muscled, and honed to perfection.

"Wow."

"All that renovating offsets the day job," he said, watching her.

"Oh, boy does, it," she whispered.

Josh chuckled and joined her on the bed, returning his attention to her breasts. Mouth, tongue, hand. All blended together to take Dana to new heights of ecstasy. She ran her hands over his back. When she moved them around to the side, he grunted and pulled away.

"Ticklish?"

"Yes, damn it."

Dana smiled but took it easy on him. Using her other hand, she slipped under his boxers and cupped him.

Josh gasped, letting go of her nipple.

"Foreplay, right?"

"You vixen." Josh pulled her hand away and moved out of reach.

"Not exactly what I was hoping for," Dana said.

In answer, Josh pulled off her panties and showed her he was worth the wait. With his tongue, with everything he had. She arched off the bed as the climax hit her, like a rolling wave of pleasure that just kept going and going and going.

She must have cried out because all of a sudden, Duffy leaped onto the bed, plastering her face with worried kisses.

"Duffy!" Dana said.

"Get off," Josh said, much gruffer than Dana. "Go back to bed." Josh put him on the floor, but Duffy jumped right back up on the bed.

"In the bathroom?"

"Definitely."

"Put his bed in there, too."

Josh returned a moment later, stopping to dig in his jeans pocket and come up with a condom.

"That," she said, trying to calm her breathing, "was fantastic." She glanced at the condom. "You were awfully sure of yourself."

"I was hopeful. Completely different."

Duffy whined from the bathroom and Josh leaned his forehead on Dana's stomach. "I knew there was a reason I don't own a dog."

"You love Duffy."

"Any other time than right now, yes."

"He'll settle down. Just give him a minute."

They waited and listened, chuckling as the whine got louder, then, way too slowly, quieter, finally disappearing.

"He's on his bed now," Dana whispered. "He'll be quiet as long as we are."

"I'm not the screamer, Miss Ricci."

She clapped a hand over her mouth. "Really?"

"Oh, yes, and it did quite a bit for my manhood."

"Yes, umm, about that manhood." She reached for him again and this time, he didn't pull away. Instead, he kissed her. Again and again, his hand doing delicious things to her breast all the while. Dana felt the excitement build again, in both of them.

"Woman—" Josh growled.

"Shhh!"

With a scowl at the bathroom door, he lowered his voice and continued. "If you keep touching me like that, I'm not going to make it long enough to give you what you asked for."

"Make me stop," she whispered.

"Ohhhh, you shouldn't have said that." He proceeded to prove that he could, indeed, make her forget what she was doing, with hands, lips, and body. All magical, all moving her back to that crescendo of desire.

He pulled away briefly to sheath himself, then centered over her, nudging her. Josh paused and looked into her eyes. "You sure you want this?"

"More than anything," she said, squirming against him. "Don't make me wait any longer."

He didn't. He plunged inside and Dana met him, taking all of him, reveling in their connection, the completeness of being together. Their slow dance quickened to a furious pace and she clutched him tightly, opening herself to him, begging him with her hips. Her second climax exploded through her, outdoing the first one. Josh joined her, pumping until neither of them could move any longer.

"All those months of wanting and wondering," he said, gasping. "Who knew it could be even better than I imagined."

"Agreed," Dana said, because she couldn't utter another

word.

"I'll be right back," Josh said. He stood and pulled the covers over Dana. "Duffy will probably be joining you in a moment."

He did, full of joy that he was back in his mistress's arms. Dana laughed and cuddled him.

Soon, Josh was back. "This threesome is going to be my life, isn't it?"

"Only for sleeping and daytime activities." Dana caressed his cheek. "The nighttime activities, well, that'll be all you and me."

"If Duffy allows." Josh chuckled, petted the dog, then tucked Dana against him, her back to his chest. Duffy curled up against her, and, for the first time in her life, Dana knew complete contentment. She didn't want to do anything, think about anything, or be anywhere other than right here, in the arms of the man she loved, with her beloved Duffy. She fell asleep wishing she could stay here forever.

Chapter Thirteen

"Josh, wake up."

Consciousness tugged at his sleep. He tried to bury it and go back to his wonderful dream of making love to Dana.

"Josh, please, you have to go."

He opened his eyes to Dana's slightly wild-looking, worried ones. Where was he? Oh, in Dana's bedroom, er, apartment. And it hadn't been a dream. They'd finally connected. Then, after a short sleep, they'd connected again. And it had been so much more than he'd imagined. He smiled.

"Wipe that cat-who-ate-the-cream look off your face. You have to go."

"Why?" He stretched and reached for Dana, fully intending to stay in this bed, with her, for the foreseeable future.

"Because. Please. I'm begging you. Get dressed and go out the back way."

He took a closer look. She had hurriedly dressed in the clothes she'd had on last night, if the askew seam of her leggings was any indication.

"What's going on, Dana?" Josh sat up as Dana tossed his clothes at him. He could hear Duffy growling out in the shop.

"Shhh. He'll hear you."

"Who?"

"Jett."

Josh shook his head. He couldn't have heard her right. "Jett? As in your ex?"

"Soon to be, yes. I hope."

That's right. The divorce wasn't final.

"Well, good." Josh pulled on his jeans. "I have a few things to say to him."

"No. You can't. You have to let me deal with him."

"Like you did with the divorce?" Josh yanked a shirt over his head.

"That was low, Joshua."

He sighed. "I know." He touched the skin beside her eyes, scrunched in worry. "I'm sorry. Really. But that man has no right to be any part of your life."

"I know Jett. If I back him up against a wall, he'll fight everything. If I want to get that divorce finalized quickly, I'm going to have to finesse things, take it gently."

"What does that mean? You going to let him back into your life after what he's done to you?" Hell no. Not if Josh had any say in the matter.

"No. I just...please. I'm begging you to leave and let me handle this. I'll call you later."

The panic on her face settled it for Josh. He didn't like it one bit, but he had to honor Dana's wishes. He wanted to have it out with her ex, but he refused to be responsible for making her more upset. Unhappy and fighting against his instincts, he left by the back door. He got in his car and was halfway to his house when it hit him.

Did she *want* to handle it or would she invite the flashy Jett back into her life? Josh's gut sank. He gulped to keep from throwing up. After last night, this had to be his insecurity talking. Didn't it?

~ ~ ~

After Josh left, Dana stared at the closed door, chewing on her lip. It would have been so easy to let Josh deal with Jett and make him go away. But this wasn't his task. It was hers. She needed to be free of Jett Sanders and his debt. Dana was the only one who knew Jett well enough to get him to sign the divorce papers without a fight. She squared her shoulders and went back out into the shop, picking up Duffy to calm him. She was due to open in ten minutes, but no way would she turn that sign from closed to open with Jett in the building.

God, why was he here?

"I never figured you for a dog-lover, darling," Jett said.

"Duffy's good company."

"Hmm." He looked around. "Nice place you have here."

Dana didn't like the way he was eyeing the place as if tallying its worth.

"It's a living. Barely." If she protested too much, she had a feeling that would pique Jett's interest as well. Anything with dollar signs attached. "Why are you here?"

He shrugged. "I came to see you. You're my wife, though you're not being very welcoming."

"We haven't been husband and wife for a long time, Jett."

"Technically, we have. Still are."

"Not for long. Divorce papers have been filed."

"Unless I contest it."

Which meant he already knew about the pending divorce. This conversation was going from bad to worse. "How'd you hear?"

"A friend."

"Wow. You still have friends in Spokane? I thought

you'd burned all those bridges when you told them all you were better than that place."

"I know people. You shouldn't have filed without telling me. That wasn't very nice, Dana."

Dana set Duffy down, and with a stern finger, reminded him to stay on his bed. She kept the counter between herself and Jett, but not because she felt physically threatened. She gripped it until her knuckles were white to stop her from harming the man in front of her. How could she have ever thought she loved him?

"You changed your phone number and never bothered to give me the new number. I waited as long as I did out of courtesy to you. If you'd reached out, we could have discussed it. Hell, I didn't even know you'd been in New York until I got a letter from a very unpleasant attorney." She ground out her response, reminding herself she needed to keep a clear head. Getting Jett to sign the divorce papers without contesting it was the primary goal here, not soothing her wounded pride.

"Ah, so they caught up to you." Her soon-to-be ex-husband stared at her without a smidge of remorse.

"Yes. You used my name. I didn't think you had that in you." She wanted to punch him. Give him a taste of what he'd put her through. Dana gripped the counter even tighter, praying it wouldn't break under the pressure.

Jett shrugged. "I didn't have good enough credit. You'd always kept your credit in good shape. It was the only option left to me."

"Getting a job and paying your own bills would have been a better option." *At least, for me it would. Come on, Jett. Man up for once. Please.*

"Well, that's water under the bridge. I'm here now and ready to help."

Help? "With what?"

"With this store. I know you bought it. I could make it so much better, starting with that name. Tangerine Treasures? Who came up with that?"

Dana clamped her lips tightly closed. She refused to be baited.

"And, since you own it, and Washington is a community property state, I own half of it."

Wait. What? No way could he get any part of her shop. Oh, God. This was her worst nightmare. She needed to call Aimi right away.

Jett picked up a miniature ship in a bottle. She itched to yank it out of his hands.

"You wouldn't be interested in selling it, would you?"

"W-what?"

Dana didn't get any further because the front door opened and—oh, God—Josh walked in. No, no, no. This was going to turn into a showdown and she was going to come out the worst of any of them.

"Hi, Dana," Josh said, smiling. "I'm on my way to the office and thought I'd stop in for a moment."

"Hello, mayor. That's,"—her voice choked as she noticed Jett eyeballing them both—" nice of you."

"How's Duffy doing this morning?"

Hearing his name, Duffy lit off his bed and around the counter to jump up Josh's legs. Josh squatted down to pet him, glancing at Jett.

"I'm sorry. This is Jett, an...old acquaintance of mine. Jett, this is Josh Morgan, mayor of Willow Bay."

Jett held out his hand as Josh stood. "Actually, I'm her husband."

Josh's eyes narrowed and Dana groaned as the look on his face turned feral. "Husband?" He spat out the word. "Really? Where've you been all this time?"

"Oh, here and there. Making deals, setting up my future.

Now, I'm ready to settle down with the missus."

Over my dead body, Dana thought, though the tension and anger emanating from Josh worried her more at the moment.

"And pay the debts you piled on Dana's shoulders?"

"Well, well," Jett said, looking at Dana. "Looks like you've been sharing our problems with the local mayor. What else have you been sharing, dear?"

"That's none of your business."

Josh's hands had curled into fists. If Dana didn't do something soon, this was going to get out of hand.

"If you don't mind, Josh, Jett and I have some things to work out. I'm not going to open on time today. Is there something I can help you with?"

He uncurled, curled, and uncurled his fists before walking past Jett to the counter. He leaned in close to Dana. "You can handle this, I know, but I won't be far away. Call if you need me." The breath of his voice, the lightest whisper, tickled Dana's cheek as he pecked it. "Don't let him get to you. And don't do anything rash." He raised his voice to its normal timbre. "Don't forget our appointment at noon."

"Appointment?"

"Yes. Budget meeting."

Oh, he was giving her an excuse to get Jett out of there if she wanted, but she really needed to settle things. "I'm not sure I'll be able to make it." She steeled herself against the pain in his eyes. "But I'll try."

He didn't argue with her. On his way out, he stopped in front of Jett. "Hurt her in any way, and you'll deal with me."

Jett actually laughed. "I think I can handle that."

With a last glance at Dana, Josh left the store and strode out of sight.

"So, you and the mayor, huh?"

"Jett, you have no right to ask questions about my life."

"I'm your—"

"You haven't been my husband since you left me for the big city, then plunked a load of debt on my doorstep. Do you have the money to pay your debts?"

"They don't need to be paid. They won't come after you. They'll just write those debts off. Everyone knows that."

"They've threatened to take my store, Jett."

"Really? I honestly thought they'd just brush it all under the table."

"Two hundred thousand dollars? That's too much to brush away. How are you going to take care of it?"

Jett looked around. "Well, I guess we could sell the store before they take it from us."

The move from simmer to blowing her top took only seconds. To hell with being nice. She'd had enough. She came around the counter. "Listen, buddy. We're getting divorced, whether you want to or not. You haven't been part of my life for over two years and you're not going to be part of it now. This is my store. Legally. And you need to get out."

"Is that any way to speak to—"

"Out!" She put the exclamation point on the word with a finger pointed at the door.

"I can see you need to calm down, so I'll leave for now. Besides, I need to start looking for work around here. But, tell me, where do we live? I'll need an address to give prospective employers."

"Out!" Dana said again. She could feel her cheeks flaming as Jett, with laughter trailing in his wake, left the store. Only then did she sink to the floor, her legs unable to hold her up any longer. Duffy joined her, licking her face.

"Oh, sweetie. I hate this so much."

~~~

Josh ran. The rain had given way to filtered sunshine, but his emotions were still a raging storm. Jett. What an ass.

Josh knew Dana needed to deal with him herself. She needed to close that book once and for all. Still, it had been the hardest thing he'd ever done, walking away from her when he could sense how stressed she was. He'd stood just out of sight, leaning against the wall, at war with himself.

Let her deal with him. She needs this.

So instead of storming back into the shop, Josh went home, changed into sweats, and hit the sand, phone at the ready.

Damn it. Why now? Was Mercury in retrograde? Or was Raven the Trickster playing with them? First, Granson and his resort. Now, Dana's ex. What was next?

Josh stopped, breathing hard. He realized he'd almost run to the next town. He glanced at his silent phone. Nothing. No text, no missed call. He shot a text off to Dana.

You okay?

Standing there, waiting, did nothing good for his mood. After several minutes, he turned back toward home and ran hard. That didn't help either. He arrived back at his house with demons still whirling around him. He showered, dressed, and drove to Tangerine Treasures. The closed sign was still out and the shop dark, so Josh went around back and knocked.

Duffy barked. After a second knock, she opened the door. Her tear-streaked cheeks were too much to bear. Josh pulled her into his arms.

"I'm so sorry, honey. I'm sorry he's putting you through this." He shut the door behind them.

"I'm not crying because I'm upset. Well, not the kind of upset you mean. I'm angry. He's such an ass." She pulled out of his arms and paced.

"Some people have a past that makes them mean. Some just are mean."

Dana swiped at her tears. "He wants half of Tangerine

Treasures."

Josh laughed, immediately stifling it when Dana stiffened. "It's not funny, Josh."

"I know," he said, holding his hands up. "He's got no right to any part of this place. This is all yours."

"It's just that…he's really good at getting what he wants. He'll find some loophole, something. He always does. He's broke. That's why he's here. I can't lose the shop, Josh. I won't." She pounded her fist into her other hand.

"He may find loopholes, but we've got hoops. Lots of them that we can jump through. Why don't you clean up and we'll go over to Connie's for lunch? We'll come up with a plan of action to boot his ass out of town and out of your life."

Dana sniffled and wiped her nose. "That sounds pretty nice."

"Good." He nudged her toward her bathroom. "I'll take Duffy out for a few minutes and when we come back, it's food and planning."

Josh kissed her. She didn't respond or resist, which worried him. He leashed Duffy and grabbed the puppy bags. "We'll be back in a few minutes."

When he returned, he fed Duffy, who then settled contentedly onto his doggie bed. Dana came out of the bathroom, having changed into jeans and another turtleneck, this one deep purple. She'd put her hair up in her signature ponytail which meant she was ready for business, not pleasure. Josh understood. They locked up and walked across the street.

"It's warmer than normal," Josh said. "Maybe we'll get an early spring and summer."

Dana nodded, head down.

Inside the diner, Connie greeted them. She took one look at Dana, told Josh she'd get their usual, quickly brought them coffee, then retreated again.

Dana hugged her cup, staring out the window. "I feel like I'm never going to get out from under him."

Josh wanted to hold her, touch her, even if it was just holding hands. But she'd pulled inside herself. He could see that in her closed posture. So he remained quiet and waited.

"He was larger than life when we started dating. And I was so flattered that he was paying attention to me. Turns out, it was the fact that I was such a hard worker that he liked, nothing else. I had a good job and he had a need for money. I see that now. Why didn't I see that back then? It would have saved me a world of hurt."

And she might still be in Spokane. They might never have met.

He gave her a few more moments, let her stare outside, seeing nothing. Then, quietly and calmly, he asked her. "What do you want?"

Dana turned to him. "I want him gone."

Good. "I'd be happy to kick his ass to the county line for you."

She smiled then, and that small change in her demeanor lifted his mood.

"No. I need to deal with this. I also need to call my attorney."

"Good. No way that man is getting another dime from you."

"I thought he'd listen to reason, though I should have known better. It's going to get nasty and mean, getting him to leave without what he came here for. I know him."

"We can do nasty." He could see his agitation rubbing off on her and tried to calm himself down. "Look, let's start with a call to your attorney friend. We need a better understanding of the legal ramifications."

"Yep. She'll help me deal with this. I was about to call

her when you showed up. I need facts before I make decisions." Dana grabbed her phone.

Lunch got delivered while Dana was on the phone with her friend. The concentration on her face was intense. When she hung up, Josh dug into his BLT, but Dana only picked at her salad. He waited, albeit a little impatiently, to hear the attorney's advice.

"It's not all bad," she finally said. "Since I bought Tangerine Treasures after we separated and we can prove that, he doesn't have a leg to stand on."

Letting out the breath he'd been holding, Josh reached across the table to cover Dana's hand with his. "That's great."

"Yes, but she hasn't made any headway getting me out of his New York debt. She's still working on it, though. The law says debt incurred while separated isn't community debt."

"Another positive."

"Except that's not going to completely exonerate me. She's researching how he managed to incur this debt in my name. That's the real question."

"You were obviously living in separate cities. Hell, separate states. He was in New York and you were here. He used your good name."

"I know, but I don't know if the courts care about any of that." Dana took a deep breath. "I'm not going to dwell on it. First things first. Getting Jett to leave Willow Bay."

"Agreed." Josh had a few ideas, but this was Dana's ball game.

She took a bite of her food, staring back out the window. "Josh, I think we need to talk to the sheriff and see if there's any legal way to get Jett to leave. Maybe he can help."

"Good thinking. Okay, we have a new plan. Finish

lunch and go talk to the sheriff."

Dana smiled, though she still played with her salad more than she ate it. He took another bite of his sandwich and heaved a huge sigh of relief. At least they had a plan. If only he could get her to eat.

Feeling lighter, he paid for lunch and they headed to city hall.

Chapter Fourteen

"There's not really much I can do without proof of wrong-doing," said Jackson Smith, Willow Bay's sheriff, running a hand over his almost non-existent hair. "He's not breaking local laws, and an argument over property in a divorce is a civil matter."

It seemed like every time a door opened, it wasn't long before it slammed shut again in Dana's face.

"Damn it, Jackson. He must have forged my signature in New York. Isn't that enough?"

"Again, I need proof and paperwork to pick him up for that. And even if I do arrest him, from everything you say, he'll be out on bail in no time. Even then, I can't legally kick him out of Willow Bay. Though I strongly suggest you file a harassment complaint. Next time he's around, you tell him you don't want him there. It's thin, but it might help get him out of your hair, at least until you can figure this out. And, we'll need an affidavit of what you've been through because of him."

Josh put his arm around Dana and she sagged into him for a minute, then began to pace. "This really sucks, you know?"

"I'm sorry, Dana," Jackson said. "I wish I could do

more to help. I can swing by frequently with the patrol car, make it clear I'm keeping an eye on the place."

"That's okay. I'm not in physical danger from Jett, and he'd be a fool to trash the place since he's trying to extort money from me." Dana reached out and shook the sheriff's hand. "Thanks anyway, for your time."

Back in the car, Josh drove the short distance to the shop and parked around back. He got out, prepared to come in with her, but Dana stopped him. "I need to get the shop open and I need some time. Please try to understand."

"I do. Really, I do." He kissed her. "I'll be over when the shop closes."

"Not tonight, Josh. I need to think."

"I'd like to help with that."

"You can't."

He wanted to argue. She saw the struggle on his face. "Okay," he said," but let's get together tomorrow morning and go over financials. Get you on track so you can stay here in town."

Dana nodded. "I guess we'd better." She wasn't looking forward to that, but Josh was right.

As Josh drove away, she almost called him back. She missed him, missed his warmth, his "it will all turn out okay" attitude. Because she sure didn't see how it could.

Duffy needed a quick walk, after which she re-opened the store. What was left of the day amounted to a few customers and a lot of worry. Later in the afternoon, Dana stepped out front for a bit of fresh air. Two familiar young boys raced by, probably headed for the ice cream store. Their parents, Betty and Mike, followed along more slowly.

"Hi," Dana said.

Mike mumbled a half-hearted hello. Betty made to stop, but he shuffled her along after their kids. Dana stared after them. What was that all about? Had she done something to alienate them? Then it hit her. This was about her part in Granson's resort. It had to be.

Shaking her head, Dana trudged across to the café. She needed something more than the half-eaten salad she'd had with Josh earlier and she could keep an eye on the shop from there. "Hi, Connie," she said as she walked in.

"Hi. Want another salad? You didn't eat much earlier."

Dana almost said yes, but stopped herself. "No, actually. I think I'll have a BLT."

Connie smiled and yelled an order back to the kitchen. "Our mayor is having a good influence on you."

She blushed and looked back across the street. "Hey, is anything going on with Betty and Mike?"

"Not that I know of. Why?"

"No real reason. They just weren't as friendly as they normally are."

Connie dried already-dry hands on her apron. "Not sure how to say this except to just come out with it. Some folks are harboring ill will about you siding with Granson and his resort. Not me. I understand you didn't know. But some folks don't see things the way I do."

Dana's blush turned scorching and she cupped her cheeks, shaking her head. Yep, just as she thought. She'd burned bridges here. "I've screwed up so bad."

"No, you haven't, kiddo."

"I've alienated people I consider friends because I was so worried about money."

Connie came around the counter and hugged her briefly. "We're all worried."

"I took it to a whole new level."

"Those *few* who are holding this against you will understand eventually. And, if not, well, they're just ignorant fools. You're good people, Dana. Charlie and I know it. The mayor certainly knows. Just give the rest time to come around."

Charlie, who sometimes helped at the café when construction was slow, brought out her sandwich to go. "Yeah, what Connie said. It will all turn out fine in the end, I'm sure."

"Thanks, Charlie." Dana smiled.

"Want to sit and chat for a while?" Connie asked.

"No. I need to get back. Thank you. I think I needed the pep talk more than the food."

Back at Tangerine Treasures, Dana took a bite of the BLT, but it tasted like cardboard. She was back at square one with some of the folks here in Willow Bay, or worse. She'd done everything wrong lately. No wonder she was struggling so much. Damn it. Maybe she should just walk away. Sell the shop and move home to Spokane. Aimi would be thrilled to have her back. So would her parents.

Her phone pinged. Josh.

Sure I can't talk you into dinner at my place tonight?

Dana glanced at the barely touched BLT.

I just picked up a sandwich and I doubt I'm good company tonight. She needed to stop feeling sorry for herself.

You'll feel better with company and I'll show you my house. Bring your sandwich.

She'd driven through the old district several times but had never seen the inside of Josh's home. Maybe the distraction would be good.

Okay.

I have to warn you. The inside's still in rough shape.

I don't mind.

Great. I'll pick you up.

How about I just meet you at your house. That way, I'll have my car.

There was a pause before he answered, but Dana wasn't in the mood for spending the night. She had too much to sort out.

Sure. Right after you close?

Perfect. See you then.

Customers came in, an elderly couple. "Oh, you have some of Shiri's work here," the woman exclaimed. "Do you sell it?"

"Yes, on consignment."

"My wife loves Shiri's work," the man said, hugging the woman beside him. "That means my wallet is in serious trouble. Is there any give in the pricing?"

"I'm afraid not. Shiri sets the prices."

"I love this one," the woman said, touching the frame of Dana's favorite painting.

"There are several along that wall. All Shiri's work."

The couple wandered down the wall, looking at all the paintings and conferring. In the end, they bought the seascape Dana wished she could afford. She was happy for them, really she was. Their love for the painting was obvious. She wrapped it carefully in white paper and plastic. They paid her and left.

The paint on the wall was more vivid where the picture had covered it and you could see the faint lines of the missing frame. Maybe Shiri would give her a replacement. She shot off an email off telling Shiri about the sale and that the check would be ready if she wanted to come by.

Dana sat staring at the blank space. That was her life. A big empty square with nothing substantial to fill it with. Except a crummy ex, a load of debt, and a town who thought she was an idiot. The one bright spot in her life was Josh. Thank God she hadn't destroyed that, too.

An hour later, after one last customer, Dana turned the sign to closed and locked the door. She had time for a shower before meeting Josh but didn't have the energy. Maybe she should cancel, even if seeing the inside of his house interested her.

No. She'd said she would be there and she would, so Dana headed for the shower. A while later, with Duffy fed and walked, she got in her car and headed out, still not sure she'd be good company.

~~~

"This is lovely, Josh," Dana said. "I can see how much you've accomplished."

"There's still a lot of rough edges. A lot to do." He'd finished the drywall in the living and dining rooms so the texturer could come next week to finish them off.

"But you can see how beautiful it's going to look. And roomy."

He laughed. "Compared to your digs, anything is roomy. Come with me." He took her hand and led her into the kitchen. "This is the next job I'm going to tackle. I could use some advice."

Dana looked around, her eyes widening. Josh knew it looked strange. High-end appliances with no place to go. He had no counters or cupboards and used a folding table to stack things on. His kitchen sink was a laundry room slop sink. And the floors were bare plywood.

"Okayyyy," Dana said.

"Yeah."

"This is worse than my setup. You've been living like this?"

Josh shrugged. "I don't cook much, so for now, it's all right."

Dana opened the fridge on Josh's collection of beer and take-out containers, mostly from Bernie's place. "You and Bernie are pretty close," she said as she closed the fridge door.

"Like brother and sister." And that was true. Josh hadn't realized how much he missed his family until befriending

Bernie.

"Never been more than that?"

"No." Josh reached for Dana and tugged her into his embrace. "Bernie and I are oil and water. We'd kill each other if we tried to make anything more of our friendship than it already is. You know Bernie."

"I do."

"And you know me."

"I like to think I do, at least a little."

"Trust me. You know me. Can you see me and Bernie together?"

Dana shook her head. "You're right. That was silly of me. It's just been a very long, depressing day."

Josh kissed her forehead and backed away. "I get it. Come on. Let's have dinner and wine. Wine makes everything better."

"Red?"

"Would I offer an Italian anything else?"

She laughed, which made Josh happy. She'd seemed so forlorn when she got here. Hell, after her day, he'd half expected her to cancel. "I'm glad you came," he said as he held a folding chair for her at the card table.

Dana held his hand briefly before he moved to his own chair. "Me, too."

He handed Dana's sandwich container to her, then grabbed the lasagna he'd snagged on the way home. Bernie, of course, had noticed the change in his mood right away.

"Finally going for it with Dana, eh?" she'd said, then hugged him. He'd grinned like a love-struck fool.

Josh handed Dana a sturdy paper plate. "Sorry. I don't have much kitchen stuff."

"Doesn't bother me."

"At least I have real silverware." He handed her a mismatched fork and knife.

Dana laughed. "How have you lived here this long without having," she waved her hands, "basic kitchenware?"

Josh shrugged. "Like I said, I don't cook much."

"Nice tablecloth, too."

"Hey, that's my best towel. And it's clean."

They both laughed as they dug into their meals, though Dana grew quieter as dinner progressed. Josh knew from experience you can only hold off thinking about things so much before they barge right back in and take over your brain.

"What am I going to do about Jett?" she said, almost to herself.

"What do you want to do?" Josh had ideas, but he was trying hard to honor Dana's request to deal with this on her own. She had a right to be done with her ex, finally, in her heart and her mind. It wasn't easy for Josh to keep his mouth shut, though. Not one bit.

"I want to leave boot prints on his ass as I kick him to the county line."

"So do I, but that's not really practical, nor will it keep you out of jail."

"I suppose. That means we have no recourse but to deal with this legally. I—" Dana's phone rang and she glanced at it. "Aimi."

"Go ahead," Josh said. "I'll clear the table."

He couldn't tell how the conversation was going, but he prayed Aimi had some ideas. When Dana hung up, there were tears on her face. "Aimi's coming."

"She is?"

"Yes. She says we're going to put up a united front and get rid of Jett once and for all. If she can get Jett to sign the papers, we can expedite the divorce. And she's pulled together legal proof that the shop is mine, not ours. But she said she wants to see his face when she tells him all this."

"I like Aimi," Josh said, relieved.

"Me, too. We've been friends since grade school. I think she knows me better than just about anyone else."

He held out the bottle. "More wine?"

"Trying to get me to stay?"

"Something like that."

"I can't. I've got Duffy."

"Next, time, bring him with you."

"If your bedroom is anything like your kitchen, I'm not staying here."

"Let me show you."

Upstairs, he looked around the room he'd hastily cleaned before Dana arrived. It was a good-sized room now, but the king-sized bed sat in the middle of it, with a dresser at the foot of the bed, a chair next to the dresser, and nothing else. "The tapers will finish this room when they come to do the downstairs."

Dana nodded, walking into the bathroom. "Wow, this is huge."

"I needed a working bathroom, so I did this first." He looked around at the finished tile and flooring, the free-standing soaker tub and the shower that could easily hold two people at once, and didn't that give him a visual he wanted to test out? Josh shook his head and looked critically at the rest of the room. The plumbing for the double sinks had been a nightmare, and this was the only room he'd finished himself. That's all it had taken to make him decide to hire out the rest of the wall work. Definitely not his forte.

"It's beautiful, Josh." She ran her hands over the gray-veined quartz, and even stooped down for a closer look at the blue and gray floor tiles. "I love this pattern."

"Thank you," he said. While the outside of his house said Victorian, he'd wanted a more modern look inside. "It took me a long time to pick these finishes. That's why I could use some help in the kitchen."

"I think you'd do just fine on your own. But I'd also be glad to offer some opinions."

"Thanks. Check out this closet."

Dana walked into the closet barely one third full of clothes. "Wow. This is bigger than my bedroom." She whirled around, laughing.

Big enough for his clothes, and hers, but it wasn't time to ask that yet. Josh reached for her and Dana threw her arms around his neck, hugging him tight. "Thanks for showing me your house. It's amazing. It will be beautiful when it's finished."

And I hope you'll share it with me. Instead of saying what his heart felt, Josh lowered his head and kissed her. Deep and full of the promises she wasn't ready to hear. His lips moved over hers, their tongues touching, lingering, tasting.

He peppered kisses in that little hollow he already knew drove her crazy.

"You taste so good," he mumbled.

"I can't stay, Josh," Dana said, even as she arched her neck to give him room.

He unwrapped her scarf and his lips followed the seam of her shirt.

Dana wound her hands through his hair. "God, you make me feel things."

"That's the idea," he said, his hand cupping the underside of her breast. Even through the shirt, he could feel her heart pounding.

With a sigh, Dana pulled back, looking around as if confused about where she was.

Josh squirmed to resituate his aching hard-on.

She clutched her arms, closing herself off.

"Not tonight, huh?"

"It's just been a rough day."

He could relax her and wanted to more than anything. But she was right. There were things she needed to sort out, and he was in this for the long haul. So if that meant another cold shower or two, Josh would do it. Anything for Dana.

"I get it," he said, running his hands along her arms, then taking her hand. "Come on, let's head back downstairs."

"I think I need to go home, Josh. I probably shouldn't have even come tonight, but thank you. You made me feel better."

"Want me to come home with you?" He knew when he said it that she'd refuse. The look in her face showed him the conflict within her. "Hey, I had to try."

Dana smiled and Josh was glad he'd been able to drag that from her.

He helped her on with her coat, tugging it tight. "Don't worry too much about Jett. We'll find a way out of this."

Dana nodded. "And Aimi will be here tomorrow, thank goodness."

"With her coming, do you want to put off getting together on the business financials?"

"I think so." Dana touched his cheek and the look of trust in her eyes almost overwhelmed him. "Thank you. I don't know what I'd do without you in my life."

He nodded, too choked up to answer, and watched as his life got in a little blue sedan and drove away.

"Sleep well, my love," he said to the red lights disappearing down the street. Then, back inside his house, he headed for a much-needed cold shower.

Chapter Fifteen

Dana saw the metallic green SUV park in front of her store, and for once, she was glad there were no customers. She raced outside, Duffy right on her heels, and barely gave her friend time to get out of the car before she pulled her into a hug.

"Whoa," Aimi said.

"Sorry," Dana said, stepping back and picking Duffy up. "It's just so good to see you. I can't believe it's been more than six months."

"Well, you're not around the corner anymore."

"I know." Dana hugged her again. "I've missed you. Come on in. Let me show you around."

Duffy barked and Dana set him down. He led the way into the shop like a proud peacock.

Inside Tangerine Treasures, Aimi surveyed the aisles. "This place is happy."

"Oh my gosh, yes. That's exactly what I tried for. Thank you for seeing it."

"I love it. I'm going to have to schedule a longer visit here. A real vacation."

"Willow Bay is wonderful. You'll love it here."

"It's got to be better than Spokane right now."

"Ugh. Still have trouble with the testosterone at the office?

"Yes. I don't get why they think, because I'm a woman, that they can give me all their grunt work. I'm starting to believe I'll never make partner there."

They'd had many long talks in Spokane and over the phone since, trying to sort out how to deal with the very male mentality at her law office.

"You could move here. Start your own practice. We've only got one attorney in town."

"I love my little condo overlooking the river. I love most of my job. Honestly, it feels like, if I leave, they win."

Dana hugged her friend. "Willow Bay was worth the move for me. I love the area, the people, even the winters here. Or, I would if I wasn't constantly worrying about the business. Come on, let's put your stuff in back, then we can chat while I keep an eye on the shop."

They passed through the rear door, Duffy running around their feet.

"Wow. You really don't have a big living area," Aimi said.

"I told you."

"Yes, but I guess I thought it would be bigger than this. Maybe I should get a hotel."

"Not on your life." Dana set Aimi's suitcase down. "Unless you mind sharing the bed with me."

"It'll be like high school sleepovers all over again. I'm fine if you are."

A few minutes later, they sat on stools behind the counter with glasses of wine.

"So, how is Jett looking these days? Aimi asked.

"As good as ever, damn it." Dana watched the sunshine brighten outside as a cloud opened up. Jett really did look great. Trendy, not a hair out of place, nice clothes. He and

Alex were two peas in a pod and Dana couldn't figure out why she'd ever entertained Alex. That kind of flash was not a part of her life anymore, and she was more than content with that.

"You at least wish he looked like life had taken a toll on him, right? I'm with you on that."

"I don't wish him ill. At least, I don't think I do. I just want him, and his debt, gone from my life."

"And that's what we're going to accomplish." Aimi took a sip of her wine. "This is good."

"Local winery. They've won several competitions with this wine."

"I can see why. I think I'll buy a case and take it back with me."

"Oh, I can have them deliver that here to the shop if you like."

"That would be great." Aimi dug into her briefcase. "Now, let's plan our attack on Mr. Jett Sanders."

"I'm so glad I reverted to my maiden name when I moved here."

"Yes, and we'll make that legal as soon as the divorce is finalized. If we can get his signature on the divorce papers, things will happen much faster."

"I don't see how that's going to happen."

"This should help." Aimi handed over some papers.

"What is this?"

"Laws and rulings. Irrefutable proof. He's not due any part of your shop, Dana. That's your livelihood and you bought it after separating, which can be easily proven."

Relief flowed through Dana's body. Tense muscles relaxed for the first time since Jett had arrived. Tears filled her eyes. "I love this place. I don't know what I'd do if I lost it."

Aimi patted her hand. "No way can he get a hold of your

baby. Now, those New York attorneys, that's a bit tougher. But we'll fight them. And, well, I have a plan. It's a bit underhanded, but it might help your situation."

"What?"

"I want to start off sweet-talking Jett a bit. Get as much information about where he's living and how to contact him as we can. Then, I want to give that information to New York. They mentioned that they'd come after you because he'd disappeared. Even their private investigator hadn't been able to find him."

"Good old slippery Jett." Dana shook her head, wondering what she'd ever seen in him. She'd loved him at one point, though, so she didn't exactly relish what his life was about to become.

"I know that face," Aimi said. "You don't like to see anyone hurting. Let him go, Dana. He's toxic and no longer your concern."

"We were married. Technically still are."

"And he doesn't give a hoot about you or what makes you happy."

"I know. I hate confrontation, but this is necessary."

"You'll get through tomorrow and your life will be so much better. Now, what say we call Jett, schedule a meeting, then close this place up and go get some dinner."

"Sounds good. Even with the sunshine, it's a quiet day."

"Quiet? Graveyards have more activity than I've seen on these streets."

Laughing, Dana locked the shop and they took Duffy for a walk. With him settled back in his bed, Dana called Jett and set up a meet for the next day. With that done, she and Aimi headed to the car for the short trip to The Square Peg. "Bernie makes the best pizza," Dana said. "I swear, I could eat it every day." In fact, she did quite a bit. Maybe she should order a salad tonight.

"Let's go, then. I'm starved and pizza sounds delicious."

And just like that, thoughts of salad flew out the window.

~~~

Josh locked up his office, more tired than hours of renovation work ever made him. He'd spent the entire day running damage control. This town needed to pull together, and Dana needed help. Between winter and the arrival of Alexander Granson, Willow Bay was grumpy. Still, he'd poked and badgered people into remembering that Dana was good people and had quickly become a helpful part of their community.

Driving past Bernie's, he saw Dana's car, so he pulled in and went inside. Dana sat in a booth at the back. The same booth she'd sat in with Granson. Had that only been a week ago? Bernie leaned against the booth, laughing at something.

"Hello, ladies," Josh said, poking Bernie in the side.

"Josh!" Dana's smile lit up the place. "Come sit down. I want you to meet Aimi."

Josh shook Dana's best friend's hand, then sat next to Dana, happy when she turned her head and gave him a kiss.

"Been a good day?" he asked.

"It's great having Aimi here."

He tucked a loose strand of hair behind her ear. "I like seeing you smile."

"You want a beer, Josh?" Bernie asked.

"Sure. Thanks." Josh looked around. "No customers?"

"It'll pick up in a while. Always does."

"Want to join us?" Dana asked Bernie.

"You bet. Be right back."

When Bernie returned, she had beer, wine, and water for herself.

"So," Josh asked. "Got a plan?"

Dana's hand tightened around his. "We're going to

confront Jett tomorrow and have it out."

"I can be there."

"Thanks, but I need to do this myself, Josh. And Aimi will be there, anyhow."

"I get that. Don't like it, but I get it."

"We're meeting him at that diner across the street from Dana's shop," Aimi said. "Figured a public place was a good idea. We'll prove to him that he owns no part of Tangerine Treasures, then get him to sign the divorce papers. And somehow, weasel out of him where he's living now so we can give that information to New York."

Josh put his arm around Dana. "You can do it. I know you can."

She nodded, but doubt lingered on her face. No, not doubt. He knew her well enough to know she didn't like having to go all mercenary on Jett.

"I could be there," Bernie said. "A united female front. We'll progesterone him into agreeing."

They all laughed, then the front door opened and a couple with a small child came in.

"That's my cue," Bernie said, standing up. "Back to work for me."

"Seriously, though," Aimi said after Bernie had walked off. "We've got a strong case. If we can get Jett to listen to reason, there's a good chance Dana will be free of him very soon."

"Now that, I can get behind," Josh said. "So, now that the plan is set, maybe we can get on to more important things." He leaned toward Aimi. "Like you telling me stories about Dana before I met her."

Aimi laughed. "You mean, like the time she was ogling a guy on the street and ran right into a door?"

"Oh, my God," Dana said, laughing. "I hit so hard, I blackened my eye."

"Ogling some guy, huh?" Josh put his arm across the back of the booth.

"Don't worry. I'd walk into plate glass ogling you," Dana said, giving him a quick, heartfelt kiss.

"Then there was that time—"

"Wait a minute, these stories can't be all about me," Dana butted in.

"Sure they can," Aimi and Josh said at the same time.

For the rest of dinner, they talked old times and new. After saying goodbye to Bernie, Josh walked them to the car. Aimi got in, but Josh held Dana back. "I believe in you, Dana. You can do this. Don't doubt yourself."

"Thanks." She chewed her lower lip until Josh kissed her.

"I wish I could take you home and show you just how much I believe in you, but that will have to wait for another day."

She laughed, leaning into him.

"What time are you meeting Jett?"

"One in the afternoon."

"Okay, I'll see you afterwards."

He waved as they pulled away, trying to hide the worry on his face. Driving home, he thought up ways to help Dana with Jett. He shouldn't. She didn't want that. Josh gripped the wheel. Damn it. He loved her. He wanted this thing with Jett gone. When Josh pulled into his garage, he noticed the lights next door. He really needed to figure out what was going on with that house. But first, Dana. Josh went inside and sat down with his phone. He had a few calls to make.

Chapter Sixteen

Dana wrung her hands together for about the hundredth time as she stared out the window of Connie's café.

"Don't you dare do that when Jett gets here," Aimi said.

She placed them palms down on the table while they waited for her soon-to-be ex, willing them to stop shaking. When the door opened, Dana jumped.

"He's here. Stop being so jittery."

Her hands in her lap, she waited for Jett to join them. He leaned down to peck her on the cheek, but she shifted away. He glared at Aimi.

"I see you've brought the big guns out. Hello, Aimi."

"I'd say it's good to see you, asshole, but I don't like to lie."

So much for making nice with him. Dana dug into Aimi's thigh under the table while Jett took off his coat and sat in a chair across the table from them. Aimi made a googly face at Dana, who laughed in spite of herself.

"What's so funny?" Jett asked, waving to Connie and ordering a cup of coffee.

"Nothing," Dana said. "Nothing at all."

"I should say not. So, are you ready to be reasonable?"

Dana fought to keep her jaw from hitting the table. Reasonable? Her? She looked at Aimi, who motioned with her head toward Jett. Dana needed to be the one to address this. She needed it for herself, her pride, her belief in herself.

She pulled the papers out. "You need to sign these, Jett."

"Divorce papers? Not unless there's an... equitable resolution of finances." He glanced through them.

"You mean like you sticking me with $200,000 of your New York debt?"

"That couldn't be helped. I needed to show I was a player to make things work there."

"Did things work? To the point where you can pay your own debts?"

He shrugged. "A few business deals went sour. It doesn't take much to rack up expenses in the city."

"But you racked them up, as you say, in my name."

"What's mine is yours, and vice versa."

"No, actually, that's not the case."

Jett frowned. "What do you mean?"

"I mean this." Dana set a page in front of him. "Precedents, law. I'm not responsible for your debt once we're separated."

Jett pushed the paper away and sat back. "But we weren't legally separated."

Dana shoved another page toward him. "Doesn't matter."

This page, citing precedent after precedent, Jett read in full.

The café's entry bell dinged and Dana glanced over to see Gladys pull her cart in, then settle in the booth closest to the door. She waved and Dana nodded her head in greeting, then turned back to Jett. He'd gone a bit pale, but it would take more than a slip of paper to get him to back off.

"You need to deal with the New York debt yourself and get my name off it, and you need to sign these divorce papers." Dana accentuated the last few words with a finger tapping the pages.

"I'm out of funds, so sorry, but no. As for the divorce, we need to negotiate how to split our property. Now, if you sell the gift shop, we can easily just split it down the middle. Unless of course, you want me here working beside you. Day after day. Month after month."

All the blood drained from Dana's face until she reminded herself. He can't do that. He has no power.

The entry bell dinged again. "Hi, Dana. The bulletin board at the grocery store looks great. Thanks for updating it." Sam said, sitting at the next table over from them.

Josh followed right behind and pulled a chair up next to Dana. God, it felt good to have him here, even if she'd asked him to stay away. Dana leaned into him and he kissed her temple.

"How's it going?"

"This is none of your business, Morgan. My *wife* and I are having a discussion."

"Correction," Aimi said with a cheesy smile. "His estranged wife and her attorney are having a discussion with him."

"Well, now his estranged wife, her attorney, and her boyfriend are having a discussion with him. And by the way, it's Mayor Morgan to you, slimebag."

"Hi, Dana. Hi, Josh." Bernie came in and stopped at their table. "Dana, good to see you. We've got to have a girl's night out soon."

One after another, people filed into the diner. Soon, it was standing room only. Each one stopped to say hi to Dana. Not Josh. Dana. She was confused. Just yesterday, she was close to a pariah in Willow Bay. What had happened that she had all these friends now?

The bell dinged again and Dana about fell off her chair when Jim, the resident pessimist, tipped his hat as he passed by. "Dana. Mayor. Nice to see you."

"What's going on here?" Jett looked at the crowd that now surrounded them, then back at Dana and Josh. "Are you trying to intimidate me? You can't do that."

"Sign the papers, Jett." Dana said, giving him one more chance.

"No."

"All righty then," Aimi said, putting an arm around Dana. "We tried, eh?"

Dana nodded, then let loose on Jett. "Just to reiterate, asshole, the divorce has been filed. You were nowhere to be found. If you intend to fight it, you'll have to contact the courts to do so. We are officially done with you."

Aimi hid her face in the paperwork she held, but Dana could see the wide grin sneaking out.

"You may be done with him, but we're not." Dana turned around to see Sheriff Smith standing there with papers of his own. Out of the corner of her eye, she saw Gladys pull her hat down, but not before the smile on her face widened.

Jackson turned to Dana. "We couldn't do anything before, but we can now." He gestured to the papers he held, then handed them over to Jett. "Seems some people in New York have been looking for you. You reneged on quite a bit of debt there."

"So? You can't put me in jail for that. I checked."

"True," Jackson said. "Do you know what I *can* put you in jail for, Mr. Sanders? Forgery."

"What are you talking about? I never forged anything."

"You forged Dana Ricci's signature on leases, loan applications, and"—Jackson pointed to the papers Jett held—" no less than ten credit card applications. We have an affidavit from your estranged wife indicating she had no knowledge of your whereabouts, nor did she sign anything related to your New York activities."

"Of course, she did." Jett looked at Dana, leaned forward and lowered his voice. "Please, Dana. Back me up or I'll go to jail. Please. I'll make good on the debt, I swear."

Dana sat back. This wasn't easy, hurting Jett. Hurting anyone. She glanced at Aimi, then Josh, then around at everyone who'd come to support her, overwhelmed at the generosity of Willow Bay folks. They could forgive and forget. Should she?

Her heart wanted to. Fear filled Jett's eyes, a first as far as Dana knew. But he'd been unwilling to make it right until threatened with jail. And she owed it to herself, and this community, to be the best person she could be. Part of that meant sticking up for herself.

"I think I'm okay waiting for the divorce to go through without your approval."

"You can't do this to me. You're my wife. You love me."

"Loved you. Past tense. And I'm not even sure about that." Dana looked at Josh. "I understand love a lot better now."

"Oh," Jackson said, digging in his back pocket. He handed a piece of paper to Dana. "Some attorney in New York faxed this to me. Said since criminal charges are being brought up against this man and you helped locate him, you are no longer liable for his debt."

Stunned, Dana couldn't move. Aimi reached for the paper, looked it over, and nodded. "He's right. You're off the hook. Though you pretty much were already. They were just being stubborn about it."

Jackson yanked Jett up to cuff him. "Jett Sanders, you

are under arrest for identity fraud and forgery." With a tip of his hat, Jackson hauled Jett out of the café, reading him his rights as they went.

The crowd erupted in applause.

Dana clapped along with them, not quite believing how her day had turned out. "How are you all here? And why?"

"Well," Jim said, settling into the chair vacated by Jett. "We may have been a little hard on you."

Dana's eyes widened.

"I said *may* have. You still jumped the gun on that resort thing."

"I know, and I'm so sorry."

Connie set a hand on Dana's shoulder. "Willow Bay folks stick together, thick or thin."

"I'm humbled. Wow. I still don't understand how you all knew I could use some support."

"A little birdie might have told us," Connie said, glancing at Josh.

"You," Dana said, reaching for Josh's hands.

"A little support can be good for the spirit. And the backbone."

"You're right. I felt safe with everyone here. I could take Jett on."

"You did it yourself. You. Don't ever forget that."

"I won't." Dana put her arms around Josh's neck and kissed him, setting off another round of applause.

"Ahem," Gladys said from the corner booth. "Now that all this frippery is done with, what's up with that resort, mayor?"

"Well," he said, standing, "since it looks like most of the town is here—and thank you for that—I can update you. First, the date is set for the first annual Beer and Chowder Festival. It'll be the fourth weekend in February. As for that overly grand resort..." Josh took a drink of water, then reached for Dana's hand. She stood and leaned into him, so he put his arm around her.

"Turns out, Granson found a legal loophole that allowed him to slip a casino permit through the system and get approved. The tribal council's lobbyists took on the capitol and that loophole is quickly being closed. I'm on my way to tell Granson now that both his casino and liquor license are on hold pending a full review. So I'd say Granson Resort is dying a slow death."

Cheers went up again at the good news.

"What're we going to do about the cannery property?" someone asked from the back of the pack. "We don't want someone else to come in and try the same thing."

"I don't know. I'm still looking into whether or not the man actually owns the property. I'll send an email update when I have more information."

Gladys rose and pulled her coat on, heading for the door. Dana went to help her. "You're not staying for something to eat?"

"Nah. I found a good half-eaten breakfast sandwich over by that fast-food place. I'm good."

"What brought you here today, then?" Dana asked. Gladys always seemed to show up when something was happening around the town.

"I just had a feeling things were going to be hopping." She patted Dana's cheek. "You're going to be just fine now, young lady. Yessir, I believe you will."

Dana glanced back at Josh and the people of Willow Bay. "I believe you're right, Gladys." When she turned back, though, Gladys was already out the door, pushing her cart along the sidewalk. Dana, overwhelmed with all that had happened in the last hour, returned to Josh's side. He slung his arm around her shoulders, his smile as wide as hers.

They chatted with folks and introduced Aimi around.

As the café emptied, Dana sank into a chair, not sure her legs could hold her any longer. Josh, Aimi, and Connie joined her.

"Looks like things turned out pretty well, eh?" Connie said.

"I still can't believe it. Everything's been turned around. I'm free of that debt." Dana reached for Connie's hand. "And the town seems to have forgiven me. I'm so grateful."

"Honey, you need to get it through your head that you're part of Willow Bay now. A local. And we take care of our own."

"I'm so glad I moved here." Dana looked at Connie, at Aimi, at Josh. "I've come home."

Josh hugged her. "You certainly have."

~~~

Josh and Dana headed for the hotel where Alexander Granson was staying, prepared to update him on the demise of his project, which Josh looked forward to more than anything, except his life with Dana. As they walked into the hotel, his phone rang.

"Hey, mayor. This is Carl Maxwell from the county assessor's office."

"Hi, Carl." Josh muted the phone to tell Dana who it was, then put it on speaker.

"You know that property you called about a few days ago? Where the cannery used to be?"

"I definitely know the property. Has anything changed?"

"A lot, and quickly. We got a deed transfer on the cannery and land."

"Ummm, what does that mean?"

"I did some checking. Turns out some guy, an Alexander Granson, had gotten the rights to the place, but only if he came up with a significant down-payment by a certain date. That date passed two days ago and the bank took control of the property. In the space of twenty-four hours, someone else bought it all."

Someone else? Who? Dana mouthed.

Josh shrugged, his gut churning. Had they held off one corporation only to have another one swoop in?" Who owns the place now?"

"Well, that's the thing. It was purchased anonymously and put in the name of Willow Bay."

Dana's eyes widened.

"The town owns it?"

"Apparently. I'll be sending you some paperwork on it to make it official."

"And you don't have any idea who purchased the land and gifted it to the town?"

"Not a one. But look for the papers in the mail."

Josh hung up and stood there, astounded at the turn of events. Willow Bay now owned that property, and it could never be turned into something they didn't want.

"I can't believe it." He stared at his phone. "Who would do something like that? That land is valued at close to a million dollars."

Dana put her arm through his and leaned into him. "Now Willow Bay can decide what to do with the property. Maybe even put in a park."

"I like that idea. Cannery Park. Though we'll have to have a vote on that. I want it to be a town decision, so I'll pull some information together and call another meeting."

"Hopefully, this one will be less confrontational."

Josh glanced around the hotel lobby. "Speaking of confrontations, should we get this over with?"

"Definitely."

They marched up to the reception desk and asked for Granson's room, renewed and ready to take him on.

"I'm sorry, mayor," the desk attendant said. "Mr.

Granson checked out a couple hours ago."

"I guess he's not going to stay and fight, then."

"He muttered something about crazy small towns."

Josh grinned. "Yep," he said, shaking the manager's hand and walking out with Dana. "That's us. Crazy."

Stopping under the awning, he turned Dana towards him. "Crazy in love."

Her eyes widened, her smile following as she touched his cheek.

"I've loved you since you first opened the doors of Tangerine Treasures, Dana Ricci."

"I think I've loved you just as long. I'm sorry it took so many months for me to recognize it. Certainly, I was attracted to you from the first moment you walked into my store."

"You have a really good poker face, then. If I'd known, it wouldn't have taken me so long to take that first step."

"Kiss, you mean." Dana smiled. "I can't believe everything's worked out. I'm free of Jett and his debt, the town is free of that stupid resort, and we're free, finally, to see where we can go."

Josh nodded. "We could go back to my place and celebrate this new freedom we have."

Laughing, Dana pulled him along to the car. "Sorry, but I've got a dog and a best friend at my place. Any celebrating will have to be champagne and companionship for now."

Somehow, with his hand in Dana's, Josh didn't mind at all.

Chapter Seventeen

"I'm going to miss you so much," Aimi said, loading her suitcase into her car.

Duffy tugged on the leash Josh held.

"Look, even Duffy wants you to stay," Dana said, handing her the box of wine she'd bought.

"I can't. I have to get back to work."

All right, but if you ever change your mind, Willow Bay's a pretty nice place to live."

Aimi looked around as the early March sunshine bathed the town with light. She took a deep breath in, then let it out slowly. "It's something to consider, but I'm not quite ready for that big of a move."

"If you're ever ready, we'll be here to help."

"Thanks." Aimi hugged her. "You're the best friend a person could ever ask for."

"You taught me to be that."

They hugged long and tight, then Dana joined Josh on the sidewalk. Aimi waved, got in her car, and drove off.

"I got used to having her around," Josh said.

Dana sighed as they watched the SUV drive out of sight.

"Want to take Duffy down to the beach?"

Dana glanced at her watch. "Sure. I don't open for

another hour."

Hand in hand, they walked past the dunes, through the soft sand, and onto the hard pack at the water's edge. Josh let Duffy off his leash and the dog raced off, scattering gulls as he went.

Following along at a slower pace, her hand cocooned in Josh's, Dana stared out at the waves, not quite willing to believe how well everything had turned out.

"You know," Josh said. "We never got around to looking at your financials."

"Joshua Morgan, you are not going to ruin my good mood. My financials are doing just fine now, but you can look at them anytime you want. I have no secrets." *Not anymore, and I'm happier for it.*

He laughed. "We'll look at them together. Even though you don't need my help, maybe I can offer some advice."

"Which I will gladly take. But not today." Dana let go of his hand and twirled around in the sand. "Today, I'm in too good of a mood."

"I bet I can make it better."

Dana stopped and watched as Josh whistled for Duffy, who came to him immediately. *How does he do that?*

All thought fled when he pulled Duffy in tight to his side and went down on one knee in the sand, holding out a small box. Dana clapped her hands over her mouth.

"I know this relationship is new, but I feel like I've loved you forever," he said. "Duffy and I talked and he's given his approval. I want to spend the rest of my life with you, Dana Ricci. I want you to pull me out of my comfort zone, make me take chances. Life will never be boring with you. Please, do me the honor of saying you'll marry me."

Duffy disentangled himself from Josh and leaped toward Dana, getting sandy paw prints all over her jeans. Dana barely noticed. She reached for Josh and he stood grasping her hand, waiting.

"Josh, you've never been boring. Not to me. Shy, maybe, but never ordinary. You make everything...brighter. You make me want to embrace life to the fullest. I can't imagine a future without you in it. Yes." She said the last word quietly, but resolutely, certain this was exactly what she wanted.

Josh whooped and pulled Dana into his arms for a kiss, and Duffy leaped all over them again. Laughing, they leashed him and headed back toward the road.

"I'm not living in that little room of yours, though," Josh said. "You two can come live with me."

"In that kitchen? No way."

Josh sighed. "I guess we'll be fast-tracking the kitchen part of the remodel."

"I guess so."

Holding hands, they walked back into town. Their town.

Willow Bay.

Home.

Epilogue

"Everything's finished. The I's are dotted and the t's crossed," the man said.

"Then the property is legally owned by Willow Bay?"

"The deed transfer was recorded today, so yes."

"Thank you, Henry. I appreciate all you do for me."

"You still don't want Willow Bay to know?"

"Lord, no. That would give everything away."

Gladys Hawthorne shut the lamp off and pushed back from the massive old desk in her study. The desk had belonged to her great-grandfather and he'd made many a lucrative deal sitting behind it. When she'd decided to settle in Willow Bay for whatever years she had left, she'd had it moved here.

Now she'd see the fruit of her endeavors blossom. The cannery would become a park everyone could enjoy. Josh and Dana would live right next door where she could watch their life together grow.

But she wasn't done, not by a long shot.

With a step much more spry than her stooped-over walks around town, Gladys poured a sherry and settled to watch some mindless television, but she couldn't quite stop the smile that spread over her face. If Willow Bay only knew...

The End

Thank you for reading **Last Resort**, the first story in the Willow Bay series. While this series can be read in any order, the next one in the series is Finding Home (Bernie's story.) If you enjoyed this book, please consider leaving a review on

Amazon, Goodreads, or wherever you prefer, and know that it would be greatly appreciated.

For new release information and news about Laurie Ryan, please join her **newsletter**.

Author's Note and Acknowledgements

During the COVID-19 pandemic, I found my happy place along the Washington Coast. Because of that, I decided I wanted to be there as much as I possibly could. What better way than to set a series there. That was the kernel that kicked off the Willow Bay series.

I made a purposeful choice not to introduce COVID-19 into this series. It's meant to lift up, to make you smile, to be a distraction, not a reminder.

As always, it takes a village to get a book to publication. To my editor, Libby Doyle, thank you, thank you, thank you! To Richard, for the amazing cover. To my critique partners, Lavada, Tricia, and Marie. I couldn't have done this without you.

And to you who've read my story, I thank you for your patronage and hope you've found something to make you smile in these pages.

Laurie Ryan

Booklist

Contemporary romance stories by Laurie Ryan

Willow Bay Series
Last Resort
Finding Home

Tropical Persuasions Series
Stolen Treasures
Pirate's Promise
Dare to Love

Standalone
Rudy's Heart
Lost and Found
Northern Lights
Healing Love
(also part of the Holiday Magic anthology)

Women's Fiction by Laurie Ryan
Show Me

Fantasy by Laurie Ryan
Survival
Enlightenment
Birthright
Awakening
Wolf's Call

Bio

Laurie Ryan writes fantasy and contemporary romance. Growing up a devoted reader, Laurie Ryan immersed herself in the diverse works of authors like Tolkien and Woodiwiss. She is passionate about every aspect of a book: beginning, middle, and end. She can't arrive to a movie five minutes late, has never been able to read the end of a book before the beginning, and is a strong believer in reading the book before seeing the movie.

Laurie lives in the beautiful Pacific Northwest, in the shadow of Mt. Rainier and a short drive to beach-walking next to the Pacific Ocean, with her handsome, he-can-fix-anything husband.

Stay in touch with the author via her newsletter or find out more at laurieryanauthor.com.

A Sneak Peek at the Second Book in the Willow Bay Series

Finding Home
by Laurie Ryan

Chapter One

The old lady pushed a tarp-covered grocery cart piled high with who knows what along the sidewalk. People driving by must wonder how her frail body managed it, but there was steel beneath her feigned fragility. This persona had served her well so far.

"Almost to the pizza joint," she mumbled. "Halfway home."

Thankfully, the May weather was moderate and patches of sunshine had graced the beaches today. The street she walked was long, one of two main roads in the oceanside town of Willow Bay. Traffic had picked up, which meant more tourists in town. Good. Willow Bay needed tourists. Barely past a long, hard winter, most of the businesses could use the pick-me-up.

For her, the day was just about over. Willow Bay had passed muster as she'd walked her route checking on the town. It was time for her to rest. She wasn't as young as she used to.

A rustling in the bushes next to the Square Peg Pizza Parlor got her attention.

"Who's there?"

The leaves stopped moving, so she pushed her cart beyond the door, out of sight of the bushes, then rounded the building and pounced, coming up with a ragamuffin teen who wore more dirt than clothes, if Gladys's eyes—and nose—were still any good.

"What are you doing in the bushes, girl?"

Startling blue eyes glared back at her as the girl remained mute.

"Well, if you won't tell me, maybe you'll tell the owner of this establishment. Come on." She grabbed her by the ear and walked her to the front of the building and inside. It was early, so there were no customers in the dining area.

She tugged the girl, who continued to glare at her, toward a chair. "Sit." Leaning over the counter, she hollered toward the kitchen. "Bernie!"

~~~

"Gladys?" Bernie came out wiping her hands on a towel, smiling when she saw the white-haired woman wrapped in layers of clothes. "I was wondering if I'd see you today. Want some pizza?"

"Nah. You gave me enough yesterday to feed me for a week, and I thank you very much for that." Gladys patted Bernie's cheek. "I brought you a stray."

Bernie leaned sideways to see behind Gladys. "A stray?"

"Yeah. You collect them, don't you? Find them homes."

"Stray animals, Gladys. Animals. Who's this?"

"I don't know. Found her rustling around outside your place. Didn't look like she was up to much good."

Bernie edged around the counter and went to stand in front of the girl. Young, maybe preteen by the look. Hard to tell through all that familiar dirt. Bernie sniffed. Been a while since the kid had bathed, too. She reached for her chin and the girl yanked her head back.

"Don't touch me."

Warning bells jangled in Bernie's head. She knew this defensive posture too well. Damn.

"What do you want to do with her?" Gladys asked, having sat herself down in a nearby chair.

Bernie watched the girl for a long moment, then took a long breath and let it out slowly, shuddering at her own memories. She should call Social Services and let them deal with the kid. That was the right thing to do. At least, that's what the law said. She knew differently and the idea of sending those angry blue eyes off to some foster home didn't sit well. Some were good, some, well, not so much. Bernie rubbed her churning stomach. She couldn't believe she was about to do this. "Leave her with me, Gladys. I have an idea or two."

"Whooeee." Gladys turned to the girl. "You're in trouble now. This one,"—she pointed at Bernie—"doesn't take shit off anyone."

Laughing, the old lady shuffled outside and both Bernie and the girl watched her shove her cart back onto the sidewalk and get on her way.

"Old bag," the girl muttered.

Bernie took a step closer, hands to hips. "I ever hear you badmouth Gladys or anyone in this town, I'll call child services to pick you up before you finish the sentence."

All attitude disappeared as fear entered the girl's wide eyes. Man, she was in a world of hurt. They both were, because it looked like Bernie had taken this little problem on. She should just call child services and be done with her.

Except Bernie knew that system personally and it destroyed kids. It wasn't meant to. It should protect them, but it was what it was.

"You hungry?"

The fear receded and a quick hit of hope filled the teen's

face before she covered it up with street swagger. "Could eat."

"Yeah. Thought so. You were rummaging in the garbage for food, right?" She didn't wait for an answer, turning to head back behind the counter. "Follow me."

In the kitchen, Bernie pointed to a door. "Wash up. I'll make you a pizza. Pepperoni?"

The girl opened her mouth, then closed it again. Finally, the war within her subsided enough for her to mumble "cheese."

"Got it. Go clean up as best you can. You can use one of the towels in there. Fifteen minutes to pizza."

The girl disappeared inside the small bathroom and Bernie slumped against the counter. What had she gotten herself into? Obviously frightened and on her own, the kid looked like she hadn't eaten in a few days. Damn it. Damn it. Damn it. That kind of gnawing hunger would drive a person to do just about anything.

Shaking her head, she made a large cheese pizza and shoved it in the oven.

When the girl came out a few minutes later, her face and hands were noticeably cleaner and her hair was hidden under a bandana. She kept her head down and sat where Bernie indicated, staring at the glass of milk in front of her.

"Yes, that's for you. And there's more if you need it."

"Th-thank you," the girl muttered with a quick glance up. She drained the glass and Bernie refilled it as a dinger went off. "That's your pizza. I'll be right back."

Bernie purposely left the girl alone, wondering if she'd run or stay for food. That she'd thanked Bernie said a lot. The kid knew how to appreciate help when she got it. It just didn't look like she'd gotten much of that for a while. Bernie attacked the hot pizza with the cutter.

Gratified that the girl had stayed, Bernie didn't

immediately set the pizza down, letting the smell of melted cheese and sauce help her gather some information. "Tit for tat. I need a name."

The girl stiffened.

"Just a first name. I can't keep calling you kid."

When she finally spoke, it was like each syllable had to be dragged out of her mouth. "I-Irene."

That was a bald-faced lie. But it was something. Bernie set the pizza down in front of *Irene* and sat across the table from her.

Irene didn't immediately dive in. She actually placed a napkin on her lap, settled her small plate front and center, then dished up a slice, covering it in parmesan cheese.

Girl likes cheese. Bernie hid a smile. "Not sure where you got Irene from, but with your permission, I'll call you Ren."

The quick jerk of the kid's head didn't go unnoticed. Ren must be close to her real name.

After she'd eaten two slices, Bernie asked the next question. "How old are you?"

That defiant chin came up again. "Old enough to take care of myself."

Yes, and she was doing such a good job of it.

"How old?"

"Sixteen."

"Bullshit. Twelve."

"I don't look twelve and you know it."

"Right around there."

There was that little jerk again. Twelve was close, so thirteen or fourteen was probably accurate.

Bernie's cell phone rang and she wrote down the takeout order as she watched the kid ate. Four pieces, then she stopped. Probably hoping to save the rest for later. On the street, food was always half now, half for the starving times. Damn, but this kid didn't deserve this. No kid did. Bernie hung her head for a moment, wondering how she was going to handle this with everything else she had going on. She couldn't put the kid out on the street. She thought about how the girl had shied away from any touch. Bernie wasn't ready to turn her in until she knew more about her story.

Decision made, Bernie stood. "Come with me. Box the pizza and bring it."

They walked outside and up the stairs on the side of the building.

"Aren't you going to lock the doors?"

"No need. This is a safe town." Bernie stopped at the door and looked at Ren. "Unless you have an accomplice?"

Ren shook her head.

"Good."

Inside Bernie's small two-bedroom, one bath apartment, Bernie took the pizza and put it in the fridge. "This is the main living space, as you can see." She tried to see it through Ren's eyes. In contrast to the dark wood of the pizza parlor below, Bernie had painted it in pastel ocean colors. The furniture was old, but comfortable. To her, it was an oasis. To Ren, it had to be heaven.

She walked down the hall, assuming the girl would follow. She did.

"Laundry room," she said, pointing to one side. "You know how to use a washer and dryer?"

Ren nodded.

"Good. I have to go back downstairs and work. You are welcome to wash your clothes." She pushed the next door open, showing the bathroom. "And you can shower and use whatever you need. Blue towels are yours."

Ren's eyes got wider.

"This closed door is my bedroom. Stay out. And don't think I won't know if you go in there, even if only to look around. Trust me, I'll know."

Opening the last door, she walked inside the small guest room. There were boxes piled up on the bed, stuff Bernie just never got around to sorting through.

"You can sleep here. Pile the boxes in front of the closet for now."

"Y-you'd let me stay?"

"Trial run. For tonight." Bernie stayed by the door so the kid didn't feel threatened, but lowered her voice to the timbre that quelled the Thompson's twins when they were tearing around her restaurant. "You betray me, you do something to lose my trust, and you're out. You got that?"

Ren nodded her head so hard Bernie almost laughed.

"All right then. Make yourself comfortable. I close at nine."

She walked out the door and downstairs to get that take-out order going, wondering the whole time what kind of huge mistake she'd just made.

Read more in Finding Home, the second book in the Willow Bay series, available at most online vendors.

Thank you for reading my book.
Laurie Ryan

Lightning Source UK Ltd.
Milton Keynes UK
UKHW010952080223
416610UK00015B/1803